THE
MAN
WHO
LIKED
TO LOOK
AT HIMSELF

THE
MAN
WHO
LIKED
TO LOOK
AT HIMSELF

K. C. Constantine

Saturday Review Press/E. P. Dutton

NEW YORK

Published simultaneously in Canada by
Doubleday Canada Ltd., Toronto

ISBN 0-8415-0266-8
PRINTED IN THE UNITED STATES OF AMERICA

THE
MAN
WHO
LIKED
TO LOOK
AT HIMSELF

THEY WERE ON the Addleman farm, one of the dozen or so farms leased by the Rocksburg Police Rod and Gun Club for the small-game season. Mario Balzic, Rocksburg chief of police, had prepared himself for more than a week for the pleasures of hunting pheasant with a dog. What he had not prepared himself for was hunting with this dog of Lieutenant Harry Minyon's, this overweight, badly conditioned, ill-tempered Weimaraner.

When Balzic thought about it, he wondered how he had let himself be fooled for a minute that the dog would be different from her master. From the first, Minyon had very clumsily masked the arrogance behind his great, florid face with a flurry of ingratiating words and promises.

"I hear you're a hunter," Minyon had said within minutes after they'd met.

Balzic had gone to Troop A Barracks of the state police as much out of courtesy to the new chief of detectives as to look him over. Such protocol was expected, and to violate it was to ask for trouble. But after five minutes with Minyon, Balzic knew he was going to miss Lieutenant Phil Moyer—

the man Minyon replaced—more than he'd ever imagined.

"Yes, I hunt," Balzic had said. "But nothing big. What I really like are pheasants. Maybe because I get lucky every once in a while and hit one."

"You know," Minyon had said, "I've got a dog."

Minyon had a way of leaning close and lowering his voice when he thought he was saying something important that gave Balzic the feeling he was talking to an insurance salesman who had taken the Dale Carnegie course out of desperation.

"You have a dog, huh?"

"I'll say. Weimaraner. Paid four hundred bucks for her. What a lady she is. What a nose. Maybe we can get together sometime," Minyon said, his large, florid face opening for the invitation. When it didn't come, he forced it. "Tell you what. Let's make it official. Opening day's only a week off. I'll pick you up, and you can show me the hot spots. I hear you fellas have a club."

"Yeah, we lease some farms and stock a few birds. Nothing big."

"Ever hunted with a dog?" Minyon said. "I mean a real dog?"

Balzic committed himself then with a simple negative motion of his head. It had been such a slight movement, he asked himself later whether he had even made it.

Now, here he was, suffering one aggravation after another, beginning with the first one in Minyon's car. Balzic had just got settled in the front seat, had taken one brief, envious glance at the dog in the back seat, and then slid his left hand up on the back of the seat. Minyon was still in low gear when the bitch reached her long, smoke-gray snout up and nipped Balzic's hand. Not hard. Just hard enough to leave teeth marks, but Minyon thought it was all very funny.

"Just her way of letting you know what's what," Minyon had said.

Balzic should have known right then.

In the field, there was one disgrace after another. The bitch flushed starlings, had to be put on the leash and led away from a groundhog's burrow, and stood baying for five minutes at a squirrel she'd treed. When Minyon finally coaxed her away from that, she'd immediately pointed another starling—only because this one had a broken wing—and Balzic, in a fit of temper at both Minyon and his dog, blew the starling apart from less than ten yards.

"Would've just starved to death anyway," Minyon said.

And Balzic, pocketing the empty and loading, wanted to turn the twenty gauge on them both, one barrel for Minyon and the other for his four-hundred-dollar bitch.

Minutes later, the bitch was into a copse of crab apples, whining, ripping back and forth through the brambles, her tongue flying and sides heaving, and Balzic could not guess what she'd come up with this time. She ignored every signal Minyon gave, and then, in what seemed a final display of contrariness, started digging in a shallow swale in the middle of the copse. Grass and dirt flew, and Balzic broke open his gun and sat in the timothy and rubbed his neck.

Minyon tried everything to get the bitch away from her digging. Nothing worked. Every time he dragged her away and started her in another direction, she wheeled around and headed back to the swale. The third time, he put the leash on her and took her nearly two hundred yards away, but the moment he unleashed her, she made a line for the copse, clawing at the same spot in a frenzy.

Balzic could hear pheasants all around. They sounded to him as though they were calling each other to come get a closer look at the two fools with the lunatic dog.

Just as Minyon reached the dog, Balzic got to his feet and started thinking of a polite way to say they ought to pack it in. At that moment, the dog took a gulping lunge in the earth and came up with what looked to Balzic from where he was to be a short stick.

The dog ducked around Minyon and took off, bounding and snarling, the stick firmly in mouth, and shot past Balzic, looking for all the world as though she wanted to give them both a chase. Then she stopped and let the stick fall between her paws.

"Play time, is it," Balzic muttered, advancing on the dog, but when he got within a few feet, the dog snatched up the stick and spun off, only to stop twenty yards or so farther away, there to turn, drop the stick, and plop on her haunches, saliva dripping from her lips, ears back, and sides billowing.

Then, as capriciously as she had run from Minyon, she picked up the stick and went loping up to him and dropped the stick at his feet.

"Good girl," Minyon said, patting the dog's head. "Good girl."

Balzic approached them, man and dog both seeming curiously smug, and had to tell himself to say nothing sarcastic. The only way to do that was to say nothing at all.

Minyon examined the stick a moment and then smelled it. "Anybody ever find any Indian burial grounds around here?" he asked as Balzic came up.

"Oh, there've been a couple. Last one I know of was over on the McKelveen farm. About two miles from here. Why? She dig up an Indian?"

"Well, this is just a guess, but this isn't any animal's bone," Minyon said, savoring his words. "And as another guess, I'd say it didn't belong to any Indian—not unless they were in the habit of sawing their people up before they went to the happy hunting grounds."

Balzic took the bone from Minyon's outstretched hand. He looked at the ends of it and then rubbed it on the grass. As the dirt came off, the saw marks were unmistakable. He held it alongside his own leg. "I'll be damned," he said. "Wasn't very big, was he?"

"Now that, I suppose, would depend on how much was sawed off," Minyon said, looking quite satisfied with himself. "Think maybe we better have a look where she was digging."

They went into the copse of crab apples and found the spot. All they could do was scrape around with the sides of their shoes and they soon saw the futility of that. Minyon called the dog over, but she just sniffed the ground a couple of times and then started barking and leaping after the bone in Balzic's hand.

"What do you think?" Balzic said, raising the bone above his head and using his knee to fend the dog off.

"I'll tell you what I think," Minyon said, his face assuming what Balzic would soon come to recognize as his professional expression, "I think you ought to run that bone over to the coroner, and I think I ought to call Hershey and tell them to send out the dogs. We could dig around here for a year, but those dogs they got, hell, they'll put us on to the right spot in a couple hours. One thing though."

"What's that?"

"Be sure to tell the coroner not to do anything to disturb the smell. Anything else he has to do, okay, but no fooling around with the smell." Minyon walked off without another word, heading for the car, and Balzic, following a half dozen steps behind, knew this was going to be the order of things if he hoped to get along with Minyon.

The new chief of detectives at Troop A hadn't thought to call his dog, and they were nearly to the car before she came trotting past Balzic. He had to tell himself that grown men don't kick dogs, or at least not for the reasons he wanted to kick this one.

Dr. Wallace Grimes always struck Balzic as being wholly unsuited to his elected job. He seemed the sort who should have been tending to miners and their families in one of the coal towns of the county, taking his pay as much in trade from the miners' gardens as from their wages. He looked to Balzic better suited to saving life than to investigating the causes of death, though Balzic could not say why he had that impression. It may have come from the deep frown

Grimes always seemed to have imprinted on his narrow face, as though he felt some part of the responsibility for the death of the corpses he had to work with.

Balzic thought about it as Grimes disappeared with the bone into the laboratory he used at Conemaugh General Hospital and decided he really had no reason for believing anything about Grimes one way or the other. He had never discussed anything personal with Grimes, and what seemed a frown of responsibility might be nothing more than an expression of professional curiosity.

Grimes was back from the lab in less than fifteen minutes. "There's much more to be done, Mario," he said, "but right now I'd say with some certainty this is the femur, the thigh bone, of an adult somewhere between five eight and six feet. As a guess, I'd say it's been in the ground between a year and eighteen months. Remember, I'm still guessing at this point, but if you can guarantee that I'll have it for another four hours, I'll be able to tell you practically to within the week it was buried."

"That's all right with me," Balzic said. "Minyon might have other ideas, but that's his problem."

"I assure you," Grimes said, his frown deepening, "I could not tell you anything really useful before four hours."

"Take whatever time you need. Just give me a call soon as you know something."

Balzic drove home to change clothes. The heavy wool shirt he'd put on under his hunting jacket in the morning was causing him to perspire freely, and he looked forward to a shower and a cold beer. He was just pulling into his driveway when the radio came on with his call signal. It was the state police.

"Lieutenant Minyon requests info regarding bone found on farm, over."

"Who the hell is this?" Balzic said.

"Sergeant Rudawski, Mario."

"Rudy, hell, man, you sound like something out of the movies." Balzic pulled on the hand brake and waited.

"What have you got, Mario?"

Balzic guessed then from Rudawski's tone that Minyon was standing close by and thought better than to kid Rudawski again. "Tell Lieutenant Minyon the coroner needs the bone for at least four more hours to make sure, but his first guess is it's the thigh bone of an adult somewhere between five eight and six feet. Probably been buried for a year to a year and a half. Over."

"Roger."

"Any word on the dogs?" Balzic said.

"Dogs on the way. Estimated time of arrival eleven hundred hours tomorrow. Repeating, ETA eleven hundred hours Thursday."

"Tell the lieutenant I'll see him then. Out," Balzic said, hanging up the mike and getting out of the car. He went up the steps of the porch to the front door and let himself in, wondering why it was that men like Minyon weren't satisfied unless they were making everybody work according to the letter of regulations. What a story they'd give you if you asked them about it—no matter what the people who worked for them would say about it. He remembered a lieutenant on Iwo Jima, an honorable-mention all-America tackle from some Big Ten school, always riding his platoon aboard ship. Two days after the landing, he remembered crawling past that lieutenant's body, face down in the black ash, with twenty-seven holes in the back of his jacket. Balzic remembered forgetting everything else to stop and count those holes. . . .

He started to shut the door and caught sight of his mother in the recliner in the living room. She was nodding, her mouth slightly ajar, the TV section of last Sunday's paper in her lap. On the screen in front of her, a pleasant-looking man was asking some cub scouts if they were ready to sing the song they'd prepared.

Balzic tiptoed over and turned the sound down and then walked softly into the kitchen. He could hear the shower running upstairs and went over to the steps and called up: "Ruth, you up there?"

Before he could tell whether he'd been heard, the phone started ringing and he bounded over to answer it before it woke his mother.

"Balzic."

"Just a moment, chief," a female voice said, "Mayor Bellotti wants to talk to you."

"Now what," Balzic said to the wall.

"Mario?"

"Right. Angelo?"

"Who else? Listen, Mario, I just wanted to make sure you were coming to council meeting tonight."

"I wasn't planning on it. Why?"

"I just had a citizen here, a Glenn Hall, who claims your people put up some no parking signs and painted a yellow line on a curb in front of a property he owns on South Main. Next to H & T Transport—you know that trucking outfit?"

"I know it," Balzic said. "But I can tell you right now my people didn't have anything to do with it. That had to come from the street department, so if the citizen has a complaint he better take it up with Councilman Maravich. He's still in charge of streets and roads—"

"Mario, a moment. Maravich says he doesn't know anything about it, besides which, Mr. Hall here claims somebody in your department has some kind of grudge against him."

"Aw, come on, Angelo."

"I know, I know," Bellotti said, "but Mr. Hall says somebody in your department is responsible."

"Well, what's the friction anyway?"

"The friction is that H & T's trucks are breaking down the curbs and making it tough for his tenants to park their cars, and his insurance company is giving him fits about—"

"Okay, Angelo, okay. Tell the citizen I'll be there tonight to officially deny that anybody in my department ordered the signs, how's that?"

"That's what I wanted to hear, Mario. See you tonight. Eight sharp."

"Right," Balzic said, hanging up. "Oh, brother."

"What was that all about?" Ruth said, tiptoeing barefoot into the kitchen with a towel wrapped turban-fashion around her hair, clutching her terry-cloth robe to keep it from falling open.

"Who knows?" Balzic said. "Some clown says one of my people has a grudge against him and put a yellow line in front of his property and stuck up some no parking signs. So now I have to go to council meeting tonight and make funny noises. It's going to be the perfect end to a perfect day."

"Was hunting bad?"

"Don't ask," Balzic said. "Listen, you're through in the shower, right?"

"No. I'm still in it," Ruth said. "I only look like I'm standing here."

"Oh, funny. I just keep running into funny people today. Minyon's bitch—that four-hundred-dollar bitch I was so goddamn anxious to get out with?—I'm not in the car five seconds and it bites me, and Minyon thinks that's very cute. He gets a real charge out of that, and now there's this citizen who thinks I go around at night painting yellow lines—"

"Aw, poor baby," Ruth said, snuggling close to Balzic, "do you want to go outside and eat some worms?"

Balzic gave her a healthy whack on her backside. "Out of my way, woman, before I really take the heat."

Ruth backed up and went into her Scarlett O'Hara act. "Why, Rhett, honey, I didn't know you felt this way." She made her eyes flutter and let out a long sigh.

"Will you be straight for a minute?" Balzic said but then had to laugh. "Okay, okay, I know when I'm licked." He went up the steps to the bathroom, unbuttoning his shirt as he went, telling himself he was lucky to have married a

woman with a sense of perspective, otherwise he could
start to like feeling sorry for himself.

The council meeting started smoothly enough and went
on that way until all the old business had been attended to.
Bids for salt for the streets for the coming winter, submitted
at a previous meeting, were approved; two zoning ordi-
nances, recommended for approval by the zoning authority,
were approved; the negotiating commission engaged in
bargaining with the garbage drivers and mechanics reported
that the new three-year contract was submitted to the rank
and file with the unreserved endorsement of the union
negotiators; and bids for sandblasting the exterior of city
hall were tabled for further study. A retirement dinner and
gift for a woman clerk in sanitation were approved by
voice vote but not entered in the minutes.

Balzic was looking at his watch for the third time in five
minutes when the meeting was opened for new business and
the chairman of the new human relations commission,
Councilman Paul Steinfeld, introduced a Reverend Luther
Callum from among the sparse group of spectators. Mayor
Bellotti agreed to let the reverend speak, and just as he
started—he opened a briefcase and took out a substantial
stack of papers—someone tapped Balzic on the shoulder.

It was Vic Stramsky, Balzic's second-shift desk sergeant.
"The coroner just dropped this off, Mario," Stramsky whispered, handing Balzic a large manila envelope.

Balzic nodded and opened it and read:

Subject: Bone examination
To: Mario Balzic, Chief of Police, Rocksburg, Pa.
From: Wallace Grimes, M.D., Coroner, Conemaugh
        County, Pa.
Copy to: Lt. Harry Minyon, Chief of Detectives, Troop
        A, Rocksburg Barracks
The bone examined by me this 18 Oct. 1970 is un-

doubtedly a left human femur. It was severed by a fine-toothed saw just below the lesser trochanter and just above where it would have joined the patella. It was also unquestionably a healthy bone at time of severance. Because of its size the assumption must be that it was the bone of a male or an unusually large female. Age of bone estimated to be between forty and fifty years. Deterioration of cells in the marrow indicates the bone was severed approximately fifteen months ago, mid or late July 1969.

So, Balzic thought, that tells us something. He looked up in time to see the reverend gesturing in his direction and saying, ". . . times in the past month, I have tried to arrange a meeting with that man, and four times I have been given a polite but clear runaround. I have yet to speak to that man, and, gentlemen, I for one am getting very weary of being told the chief is out, the chief is busy, the chief is working on this, that, or the other case. That, gentlemen, is why I bring my case to you tonight.

"Three instances, gentlemen," the reverend went on, "three in the past six weeks of clear and unmistakable harassment of black juveniles for no other reason apparently than that they were on the streets after midnight and, though I hesitate to say it, gentlemen, that they were black."

Balzic put the coroner's report back in the envelope, let out a very audible sigh, and started looking around for an ash tray.

"The chief may sigh all he wants, gentlemen," Reverend Callum said, "but facts are facts, and I have the documented facts here in my hand." He held up the papers in his hand and then went to the table where the mayor and the four other members of city council were sitting and began to pass out copies.

Balzic found an ash tray and, after lighting a cigarette, put up his hand. Mayor Bellotti recognized him just as

Reverend Callum handed out a set of papers to the last councilman.

"Mr. Chairman," Balzic began, but was immediately interrupted by Reverend Callum.

"Mr. Chairman, I didn't relinquish the floor. I still have plenty of things to say—"

"All I wanted to ask," Balzic said, "was if you had a copy of those facts for me, that's all."

"Well if you'll check downstairs in your headquarters, chief, you'll find you already have several copies, because every time I tried to see you and was told you weren't in or were busy or whatever, I left you a copy."

"Yeah, well, for right now, do you mind passing me over a copy?"

"Not at all," Reverend Callum said, handing a copy to one of the spectators to pass back to Balzic. The reverend could not restrain himself; he had to smile at his triumph.

Balzic tried to ignore the reverend's smile as he reached for the copy but found his face tightening anyway. He scanned the pages, looking for names, and found two that brought situations quickly to mind. "Mr. Chairman," he said, "I can settle a couple things right now. For instance, this James Ronnie Dawson, listed in the reverend's report as a juvenile, is not a juvenile—"

"The Dawson case," Reverend Callum said, "is a classic example of police harassment of members of minority groups—"

"Will you wait a minute," Balzic said. "I'm trying to tell you something, man, that you need to know. Just answer me one question first, will you, please?"

"I'll be more than happy to extend the courtesy to you, a courtesy, I must say, you have never extended to me."

Balzic let that go and asked, "How long you been in Rocksburg?"

"I resent your implication," the reverend said. "You're implying that because I'm new here in your city, I'm something of an outsider. The outsider is invariably the scapegoat for all problems, especially racial problems. When you've got a problem that suddenly is brought to light—never mind that it has existed all along—it is because some outsider came in and stirred up the residents. Well, it may be true that I am new in my ministry here—"

"How new?" Balzic said.

"I accepted the call here five months ago."

"That was simple enough," Balzic said, doing his best not to smile. "Now, what I want to tell you is this Dawson, this guy you claim is a juvenile, is, in fact, twenty-three years old. The reason I know that is I personally checked his birth certificate with the state because every time he gets in trouble, not only here but in Pittsburgh and Erie, among other places, he's always using the line that he's a juvenile.

"But the facts, reverend, facts you don't have on these pages as far as I can see, are that Dawson has a yellow sheet dating back to age thirteen, everything from truancy to auto theft, and on the night you have down here, September seventeen, Dawson was arrested on suspicion of burglary, and when he was apprehended he, uh, resisted arrest, to say the least. The fact is he put up one helluva fight before he was subdued, and when he was finally subdued, he was found to be carrying a twenty-five-caliber automatic.

"I was present at his arraignment, and he was booked on charges of resisting arrest and violating the firearms act. Two days after he was remanded to Southern Regional Correctional, he was released on five-thousand-dollar bond, a bond I argued against for all the reasons you can think of. As a matter of fact, I got a call from the narcotics division of the Pittsburgh police yesterday, asking me what I knew about him. It seems they picked him up and he just happened to be carrying about seven, eight hundred Benzedrine tablets on him in a paper bag and gave them the story that he was working for a drugstore as a delivery boy.

"As for this Maurice Williams," Balzic continued, talking fast so as not to be interrupted, "well, his story isn't too much different except that he *is* a juvenile—I think he just turned eighteen—but he also has a yellow sheet going back five or six years, only the charges against him are mostly assault in one form or another, including one against his mother and one against his stepsister. Then there was the complaint made by his stepsister for rape, and the date you have down here, October first, is the day we picked him up for assaulting his stepsister, which was two days after she'd made the complaint against him for rape. And when we did pick him up, we also brought in his sister, and I have photographs downstairs, reverend, if you want to see them, of the way his stepsister looked that night. That was also the night the stepsister dropped the complaint of rape against him. We booked him for assault and battery and aggravated assault, and a couple, three days later, somebody posted bond for him. So he's out on the streets now, and I guarantee within a month, six weeks at the most, somebody else is going to get hurt.

"Now, as for the third instance, this Roland Bivins, I have to tell you straight, his name doesn't ring any bells with me, and I'd like to have time to check it out. That's all I have to say now, Mr. Chairman," Balzic said, and sat down, putting the ash tray in his lap. He stood again and said, "One more thing, Mr. Chairman, I have to apologize for this, because it is true that I knew the reverend was trying to see me, but I did have other things to do, things which seemed more important to me at the times he wanted to see me, and I probably should've made the time to see him, if for no other reason than to save everybody a lot of time in this meeting."

Mayor Bellotti nodded to Balzic and said, "Reverend Callum, I don't doubt your sincerity for a minute, and I give you my word that we're going to read your report, but I think I speak for all the council here when I say the best thing is for you and Chief Balzic to get together and iron this thing out. And I'll be happy to make a resolution to that effect and somebody else can second it. . . ."

While council decided about the resolution, Balzic

studied the Reverend Callum. The reverend looked suddenly a disillusioned young man, and Balzic, as much as he thought he ought to be annoyed about the whole thing, could not help feeling sympathetic for the way Dawson and Williams had gulled him. It was very easy to be lied to when you had as much faith in a conviction as the reverend obviously had. Of course, Balzic had to admit that because he knew nothing about this Roland Bivins, the reverend might well have a case there. Balzic knew there was more than one man on his force who hated blacks on sight. He thought he had succeeded in keeping them out of the blacks' district, but the chances were probably no better than even that he'd missed somehow and sent the wrong man on the wrong beat.

The resolution was made, seconded, and approved without dissent, and Balzic was directed to meet with Reverend Callum at their earliest convenience. The reverend expressed his satisfaction to council, though Balzic thought the reverend's face showed more resignation than satisfaction.

The Reverend Callum had no sooner found his seat than a short, paunchy man with diminishing hair and wearing an expensive suit jumped to his feet and demanded to be heard. He turned out to be Glenn Hall, and, after a series of exchanges among Mayor Bellotti, Councilman Joe Maravich, and Hall, most of them concerned with whether Hall was out of order, it was agreed to let Hall speak his piece. He went into a long, rambling tirade about the yellow lines and no parking signs in front of his property on South Main, a situation he said reduced itself to the city providing a free parking lot for the trucks of H & T Transport, which in turn was causing the curbs and sidewalks in front of his property to crumble, causing his insurance company to raise his rates, and causing his tenants in the four-apartment building to pester him to death with pleas for relief, and on and on.

Balzic listened half attentively until Hall made the charge that someone in the police department had a grudge against him and had put the yellow line on the curb and the no parking signs up as a way of "getting" him.

"That's ridiculous," Balzic said, without either standing or asking to be recognized.

"That's what you say," Hall shouted.

"I think Councilman Maravich ought to reply to this," Balzic said. "He has more to say about restricted parking than anybody in the police department ever had or has. As far as I know, any time my department wants to have a parking zone changed, we still have to apply to the streets and roads department. Hell, I've been trying to get Burroughs Street made one way for five years now, and I haven't been able to convince Mr. Maravich that it's necessary. Just how in the hell could I restrict parking in front of your place without first going through a formal application in a public meeting?"

"Well that's exactly what I'm trying to tell you," Hall shouted. "It wasn't done in a meeting. It wasn't done in public. It was done in some backhanded—"

"Now wait just a goddamn minute," Councilman Maravich said. "I admit that my clerks are having a little trouble finding the original requisition for that parking restriction, but I've been doing a little checking myself. Number one, the mortgage of the property you're talking about is held by Rocksburg Savings and Loan, and the property you're complaining about—H & T Transport—also happens to be mortgaged by Rocksburg Savings and Loan. . . ."

Balzic's mind began to wander then. He knew what was coming—a long, tedious explanation about the possibilities of mortgage payers competing with each other for special favors from mortgage holders—and he wasn't particularly interested in any of it. He had had his say, brief as it was, and he knew the whole thing would be settled out of his hands anyway.

His mind was going back to the envelope on his lap, to the bone, the left femur of the male or unusually large female, age forty to fifty, severed and buried some fifteen months ago. He searched his memory for someone being reported missing. Nothing. He thought about the place, the Addleman farm. Nothing there either.

The woman, Mrs. Addleman—he couldn't remember her first name—lived there with her invalid mother. He had seen them both that morning when he'd gone up to the house to tell her that he and Minyon were going to hunt on the place. Mrs. Addleman was just pushing her mother's bed over to the sun window in the living room when Balzic walked up on the porch, and the old woman had waved at him through the window.

Howard Addleman had been a member of the Rocksburg Rod and Gun Club, and, in fact, had been the spokesman for a group of farmers who approached the club with the idea of leasing their land to the club for small-game hunting. But Howard Addleman had died two years ago, and Balzic recalled clearly going to the funeral home to pay his respects. Addleman was a short, burly figure even in death, a strong, quiet man whose only vice had been chewing tobacco and who seldom smiled except when somebody made a difficult shot. The rest of the time, he seemed not to enjoy himself, but Balzic knew him well enough to know that he reserved his emotions, saved them almost, as though he was fearful of wasting them on things that didn't deserve more than mere interest or curiosity.

So there was nothing there. But there had to be something somewhere.

". . . so what I'm suggesting to you, Mr. Hall, is unless you have proof of what you're saying, you better be careful what you go around accusing people of," Councilman Maravich was saying, and Balzic thought he ought to be paying attention again.

Glenn Hall reached behind him on his chair for his raincoat. He left the meeting then without another word, giving Balzic a heavy glare as he passed him, a look with a "just-you-wait-buster" menace to it. Balzic halfheartedly told himself to look into it. Who knew? Somebody in his department might be married to this guy's cousin or something. There were thousands of reasons for people to be angry with the police, most of them imagined out of proportion to the facts, but Hall might have one that wasn't. And if somebody in his department was married to his cousin and not treating her right—well, Balzic thought, there were people mad at the police for less nutty reasons than that. . . .

Balzic caught Mayor Bellotti's eye and asked him with a couple of gestures—the finger tips pressed together, palm up—if it was all right if he left. The mayor nodded, and Balzic slipped out of the council room and went downstairs to police headquarters.

Sergeant Vic Stramsky was hammering away at a typewriter, stopping after every five or six violent jabs at the keys to roll the paper and erase a mistake.

"What's that?" Balzic said, standing behind Stamsky and trying to read over Stramsky's shoulder.

"A letter to my insurance company," Stramsky said, blowing away the grit from the erasure.

"What did they do to you now?"

"It's what they won't do, the bastards. They want my payments on the button, brother, but try to get them to send a check."

"You mean this is still the same thing? Hell, that was six weeks ago."

"Seven weeks and two days," Stramsky said, jabbing away again.

"Good luck," Balzic said, walking back to the coffee urn and pouring himself a cup. "Hey, Vic, you know a guy named Hall? Short guy, about forty, getting a little thin on top, talks loud?"

"Shouts, you mean?"

"Yeah. Wears pretty flashy clothes."

"Yeah. I know him. He's a pain in the ass. What about him?"

"Anybody here got anything against him?"

"No more than you have against any pain in the ass. Is that what he says?"

"Yeah. Upstairs in the council meeting he was saying somebody down here had a grudge and ordered a yellow line in front of his property."

"Ah, he's goofy. One time, I don't know, must've been a year ago, I was in the bowling alleys, having a couple beers, you know, and he comes in and starts hollering that I tagged his car. I just look at him. Finally I say, 'Hey, pal, I haven't tagged a car—anybody's car—in four years,' and he calls me a liar. I mean, right there, in front of my brother and his wife's cousin and about twenty other guys. I had to leave. If I'd've stayed, I don't know . . ."

"Well what's with him?"

"Who knows? I heard, I don't know how true it is, but I heard one time he went all the way to the state finals in wrestling in high school and got his ass whipped. Maybe he's still trying to win that one."

Balzic thought that over and then asked, "Anything happening tonight?"

Stramsky shook his head. Then he wheeled around suddenly in his chair, his face beaming. "Hey, I didn't tell you. Got two ringnecks today! Two!"

Balzic turned his back on Stramsky and stared out the window and watched traffic on Main Street.

"What's the matter with you?" Stramsky said.

"I was out today," Balzic said. "With Lieutenant Harry Minyon. All I got was a starling with a busted wing and a goddamn bone."

The dogs arrived a half hour early. Six bloodhounds with their three handlers, and Balzic thought he saw a faint resemblance between dogs and handlers, a long-faced, sad-eyed impatience to get on with the job.

Lieutenant Minyon, in uniform, came in the lead car and

parked beside Balzic in the front of the Addleman barn, a
building beginning to develop a saddle in its roof.

"You have the bone, I hope," Minyon said.

Balzic produced it, still wrapped in plastic, from the front
seat of his car.

"You told him not to foul up the smell?"

Balzic nodded. "I told him. Whether he did or not isn't
for me to say. Maybe the dogs'll know."

"Can't tell you how surprised I was to find out Grimes
was an M.D.," Minyon said. "Most of these small county
coroners aren't."

"Grimes is a good man," Balzic said, and let it go at that.
He was going to add that Grimes had been a pathologist
in a large university hospital in Philadelphia for years before he'd moved here, but he didn't feel like getting into
anything with Minyon this early in the day, or in the case,
for that matter.

Minyon looked the dogs and handlers over to see whether
they were ready and then set off toward the copse of crab
apples where they'd found the bone. They had to pass
through what had been prime pasture when Howard Addleman was alive and tending his dairy herd. It was flat
for the first couple of hundred yards and then started ris-
ing. Minyon set a brisk pace, and for the first few minutes
was far ahead of the rest, but by the time they crested the
small hill, he had fallen off his pace so that Balzic could
hear his breathing. Minyon's dress uniform hadn't made the
pace any easier. Circles of sweat were starting to show on
his tunic under his arms and in the middle of his back.

"Right down there," Minyon said, stopping to tell the
dog handlers and to point at the copse of crab apples. "What
I think is you ought to let the dogs get the smell of the
place first before we let them have a sniff of the bone."

If the dog handlers objected to Minyon's plan, they gave
no indication of it. The more Balzic looked at them, the
more they came to resemble the taciturn and docile man-
ner of their dogs. But there was something about them,

something just under the surface that belied the surface, something that said to Balzic they were going to conduct their search the way they wanted, no matter who was giving what orders.

The search began around noon Thursday and lasted as long as there was daylight until afternoon Monday. Dogs and men covered six farms, each abutting the other and three abutting the Addleman farm, an area totaling nearly seven hundred acres. Each day's search produced part of a bone except for Sunday, when three parts were found, and each day the parts were turned over to Coroner Grimes. When the handlers agreed to a man that the dogs were exhausted—even Minyon admitted the dogs' foot pads were in dangerous shape—they packed them in and headed back to Hershey.

Minyon was frustrated to say the least. Furious might have been a better word for it, Balzic thought.

"They looked at me like they knew their business," Balzic said to Minyon as they were about to enter the tiny cubicle Wallace Grimes used for an office in Conemaugh General Hospital.

"Hell, man, a search is a search," Minyon snapped. "You don't stop until you've got all the pieces."

Balzic was going to say that he thought they'd got as much as they could hope to get, given the condition of the dogs, but thought saying anything to Minyon at this point was a waste of words.

Grimes was sitting behind his desk when they came in, his fingers pressed together and his eyes wide in thought.

"Afternoon," Minyon said. "Well, what have you got?"

"I was about to ask you the same thing. Not that we need much more," Grimes said. "I mean, not to determine that what we have all fits the same person."

"How about identification? What about that?" Minyon said. "Without that, what do we have?"

"Let's see," Grimes said, picking up a report scrawled in his own hand. "We have both femurs, sawed in practically the same place. We have both left and right humerus, left and right ulna and radius, and the right tibia and fibula, each severed in pretty much the same place as its opposite —excepting the tibia and fibula of course—and with unquestionably the same kind of instrument."

"Two arms, two thighs, and one calf," Minyon said. "Wonderful. And all you can tell us is that they're all from the same body. A male or an unusually large female, I think you said."

"That's right," Grimes said. "Between forty and fifty, dismembered approximately fifteen months ago, unquestionably healthy when dismembered. That's as much as I can tell you. That's as much as anybody could tell you. And I won't be able to tell you any more than that unless, of course, the skull is found, hopefully with the teeth still in place. If we had that, it would simplify matters considerably."

"Yeah. Well, we don't," Minyon said. He shoved some papers away from the corner of Grimes's desk and sat on it. Grimes frowned his disapproval but said nothing, instead arranging the papers nearer to him. "And nobody's found anything in any of the dumps or landfills either," Minyon added. "How much water is there around here?"

"A helluva lot," Balzic said. "I wouldn't want to start dragging it. Tough enough when somebody drowns and we know where they drowned. I'd hate to have to tell a bunch of divers they got to find pieces when nobody even has the first idea which water to start in."

"Then just what the hell do you suggest?" Minyon said.

"Well, it wouldn't be a bad idea to start going over the membership list of the Rod and Gun Club."

"Why?"

"Because all those farms where we found what we've found were leased by the club. Somebody had to be familiar with them."

"Well why in hell didn't you say this before?" Minyon said.

"You didn't ask before," Balzic said, swallowing once to get the phlegm down.

"How many other farms are there?"

"I'm not sure. Six. Eight, maybe more. I used to be involved a lot more with the club than I am now. I don't often even go to meetings now. Vic Stramsky is treasurer. He'd know for sure."

"A Polack," Minyon said. "Jesus, I thought I'd seen the last of them when I left Wilkes-Barre."

Balzic walked out into the hall, knowing that if he stayed in the room with Minyon one more second, he was going to say something he'd doubtless regret.

"Where are you going?" Minyon called out.

"I'm going to see Sergeant Stramsky," Balzic said, pronouncing "sergeant" very explicitly.

"He one of your men?"

"Yes," Balzic said. He did not wait for another exchange but walked quickly down the corridor to the exit leading to the parking lot. He laid rubber pulling out just as Minyon came barging through the door waving his arms and shouting something Balzic did not bother to try to acknowledge.

Balzic parked in the alley behind Vic Stramsky's small frame house in South Rocksburg and made his way around the garbage cans and up the walk to the door leading into Stramsky's kitchen. Stramsky, barefoot and wearing faded denims, answered the knock and let Balzic in with barely a nod and something akin to a grunt. His eyes were bloodshot and the left side of his face was red and creased. He returned to a black cast-iron pan on the stove where he was frying kolbassi and peppers and onions, motioning to Balzic to pour himself some coffee. Then he broke a couple eggs in a small red bowl and began to beat them, pouring in some buttermilk as he did.

"You look like you had a good one last night, Vic," Balzic said, sipping his coffee.

"My brother . . . him and his wife's cousin came out to go hunting and they hung around for me until I got off.

They were into the beer pretty good, and when I got here they broke out the bourbon. Jesus . . . I didn't get to sleep until about five. Just woke up a little while ago. Those goofy bastards, they drove home. That isn't what you came to tell me, is it? I mean, nothing about my brother?"

"Nah. I came down to check the membership list for the club."

"What for?" Stramsky said, pouring the beaten eggs and buttermilk into the pan. He turned the gas down and worked the eggs around with a wooden spoon.

"It's about the bones. We found them all on club farms, and I'm just trying to put two and two together."

"You don't sound too goddamn excited about it."

"It's that goddamn Minyon. I don't know what it is with him, but the thought of working with him for the next three years doesn't exactly make my day."

"You mind if I eat first, or do I got to get the list for you now?"

"Hell, take your time. The sooner you give them to me, the sooner I have to get back beside that overstuffed egomaniac."

"All pumped full of piss and vinegar, huh?"

"That's him. Minyon—what kind of name is that?"

"Christ, could be couple things. Could be French. Could be dago, too. Lots of them around. How's he spell it? The dagos I know spell it m-i-n-g-n-o-n-a—something like that."

"Nah. He's no dago. I know a dago when I see one."

"Oh sure. The Pope and Rocky Graziano, they look like twins. You act like there ain't any arrogant wops around," Stramsky said, spooning the eggs onto a dish.

"Who you talking to? Man, I've seen every breed of dago there is, from my mother to Dom Muscotti and all the ones in between," Balzic said, sniffing. "Hey, that smells pretty good."

"Eat your heart out. Polack soul food, that's what this is. Them niggers can have it, so can us Polacks." Stramsky started to eat, swallowed a mouthful, and then said, "You know my brother and me were talking about that last night. You hear all these jokes about Polacks now, but you don't hear no jokes about niggers any more. Who's the groom at the Polish wedding? He's the one in the clean bowling shirt, he's the one with the new bowling shoes, ha, ha, ha. 'Bout time somebody started a Polack anti-defamation league."

"Maybe," Balzic said, "but who would you get to write the charter?"

"Oh, that's funny," Stramsky said, diving into his eggs again, saying nothing until he'd finished and put the dish, utensils, and pan into the sink and run hot water over them. Then he went into another room and returned in a couple of minutes with a large loose-leaf notebook. He handed it to Balzic. "All in there," he said. "The founders, charter members, paid-up members, plus the ones that still owe for this season, which includes you."

"Yeah, well," Balzic said, opening the book, "I'm good for it."

"Don't it ever bother you? I mean, don't it ever get to you once in a while?"

"What?"

"Owing people."

"Never has so far. I always pay."

"Christ, it drives me nuts. I can't stand to owe somebody for a week. Anybody."

"Well, that's your problem," Balzic said, skimming over the list of names. "You know, there's a helluva lot of names in here I don't recognize."

"If you'd come around once in a while, maybe you would."

"I guess. Listen. Save me a lot of time. How do you mark the ones that quit or died?"

"I just draw a line through the name. The ones with the small check beside them still owe this year's dues."

"I see I'm not alone."

"That reminds me. I got to get some stamps today. Send

out second notices. I don't see how you guys can feel right out there, knowing you owe for the privilege."

Balzic snorted. "Who's this Louis Amato? He quit or die?"

"Moved. Ohio someplace."

"What about this Francis Banaczak?"

"That was Frankie Banaczak. You remember him. Got killed on the turnpike last year."

"Oh yeah. What happened with his wife?"

"She's supposed to be going a little nutty. Least that's what I hear. Probably just gossip." Stramsky stood and poured more coffee.

"How 'bout this one—Edward Corpin?"

"Got transferred. U. S. Steel sent him to Birmingham."

"Anthony DeRamo? That's not Crackers, is it?"

"Yeah. His old lady made him quit."

"Boy, there's one for you. I remember him when he was the biggest skin hound in Norwood. I'll bet it's been five years since I've even seen him."

"He's walking straight now. Talking straighter."

"Shit, don't believe it. He'll make a comeback. He'll get the urge again. Just give him time. Who's this Gallic? Frank Gallic?"

"That's the butcher. Owns a freezer beef place south of here. Close to the river. You know him."

"I don't think so. At least I can't place him. Well?"

"Well what?"

"He quit or die or what?"

"Quit. Said he was going to a pheasant preserve up around Indiana. You know, they charge by the bird."

"I'm starting to place him now," Balzic said. "Wasn't he the guy got his picture in the paper couple times? Shot a polar bear or something. Then another time he got a Kodiak."

"That's him. He went to Africa once, too, and something tells me he also went to Mexico. Big-game hunter. Went with a couple other guys."

Balzic made a note of Gallic's name and address. "Is his

place on Route three thirty-one or fifty-one? It's typed over here."

"Three thirty-one. Backed right up against the river. Used to brag how he could fish right off his property. You know his partner for sure. Mike, let me think, Mike, starts with an 's.'"

"Samarra?"

"Yeah, that's him. The one they call Mickey, Mizzo, something."

"Hell, I know Mickey from way back. But I didn't even know what business he was in, never mind who he was partners with. Last I heard he had a store up in Norwood, but I never dealt there."

"Oh, hell, Mario, him and Gallic been partners ever since they got out of the Army after World War Two. Sure. First, they had a grocery up in Norwood. Then they got a butcher shop and grocery on the other hill across from the old Mother of Sorrows grade school. The one they tore down. Then about ten years ago they went into this freezer beef thing. All they sell is halves and quarters, you know, real cheap, but you got to buy at least a quarter or a half."

"What's the name of their place?"

"Galsam's. They took the first three letters of their last names and put them together. Just go straight south on three thirty-one till it starts to run along the river and then start looking. About six miles, maybe seven. There's nothing around it. Just the place and a couple house trailers."

"Gallic's a World War Two vet, you said. That would make him somewhere between forty and fifty, right?"

"Yeah, he'd be about forty-five or so."

"Okay. So what about this Ippolitto?"

"Is his name still in there? Hell, he died three years ago."

"Janeski. Richard Janeski."

"He's one of Gallic's buddies. One of the guys went to Alaska with him. He quit. Said he was going with Gallic to that place by Indiana. Just as well. Real contrary bastard.

Got a real bad face. All screwed up from some kind of accident when he was a kid."

"How long ago did he quit?"

"End of last season. Same time Gallic did. No, wait a minute. Gallic quit before. Yeah, he quit before last season started. I don't remember when exactly, but it was before, I'm sure of that. Janeski quit after."

"Janeski's address right? Rear 214, Church Street?"

"Unless he moved."

"Okay. What about Henry Kozal? Is that the old man—Hank?"

"Yeah. Poor bastard. He just sort of sits around now and drinks a lot. I didn't even bother sending him a first notice. Christ, first his wife and then his kid. That had to be rough."

"Somebody said his kid got the Silver Star in Vietnam."

"I don't know about that. Louie Antal went up to the house one day, see how he was doing, and the poor bastard was just sitting in the kitchen, stoned, with the flag in his lap. Just sitting there. Wouldn't even talk to Louie."

"His kid was pretty old, wasn't he? I mean, he was career Army if I remember right."

"Not so old. Thirty maybe. But he was career Army, yeah."

"Yeah, well—what about this one? Mumai. Theodore."

"He's another one got transferred to Birmingham."

"Peluzzi. How about him?"

"Another one of Gallic's honchos. You know him."

"I know Freddie Peluzzi, the bartender in the Sons of Italy, but this one, Axal, I don't."

"This one ain't like Freddie. Just the opposite. A real prick. You have to remember him. We picked him up couple times for beating hell out of his wife. The last time, it was back in sixty-six, he did ninety days."

"Oh yeah. Now I got him. What happened with her?"

"She finally wised up and dumped him. She's still around. Waits tables down the SOI Saturdays and Sundays. I don't know what she does the rest of the time."

"She the one used to be a blonde? She let her hair grow in black again?"

"Yeah. Rose, Rose Mary, something."

"Didn't he have a nickname? This Axal doesn't register with me."

"Wheels."

"Ah, that's why I couldn't place him. Now I got him for sure," Balzic said. "Wheels Peluzzi. He's another buddy of Gallic's, you said."

"Yeah. Him and Janeski and Gallic. Three of a kind. All big-game hunters. All had trouble with women. Janeski's wife is still collecting child support, from what I hear. I shouldn't say that about Gallic though. I don't even think he was ever married. Somebody said he was messing around with Mike Samarra's sister. She used to work for them. Cashier. Maybe she still does. But that doesn't sound right to me. I mean, I don't think Samarra would've gone for that."

"Why's that?"

"I don't know for sure, understand. What little I knew of him, he was a funny guy. Kept to himself pretty much. Didn't drink, didn't smoke. A bachelor. About the only thing he did that was out of the ordinary was sing."

"Yeah, he had a helluva voice all right."

"I never heard about him being in any kind of trouble, and like I said, I only saw him a couple times, but he gave me the impression he was a guy you didn't fool with. You know the breed—one of those old-school dagos. Real religious, and you don't mess around with their sisters. Hell, Mario, you know the breed better than I do."

"I knew his old man was like that, so I guess it figures he'd be like that."

"Well, that's what I'm saying. I mean, I can see him having a business with Gallic, but I can't see him letting Gallic fool around with his kid sister."

"You know her?"

"I met her a couple times. Tough-looking little broad. Looked like him in the face. Short, but built good. Little

on the stocky side. Course it's been a while since I've seen
her. Any of them for that matter. Can't remember how long
ago it's been since I've seen Mike. And I haven't seen Gallic
or Janeski or Peluzzi since they told me they were quitting
the club."

"This address still right for Peluzzi? Box 12, Pine Hollow
Road?"

"I can't say, Mario. He moves around a lot."

"Where do these two work—Janeski and Peluzzi—case
I don't catch them at home?"

"Janeski's a steamfitter down at the can factory. Peluzzi, I
got no idea. He used to be a brakeman for the PC&Y, but
you know how those railroads are. Might still be with them."

"They about the same age?"

"No. Janeski's younger. Maybe thirty-five. But Peluzzi's
got to be around forty-five, forty-six."

"Okay, what about this Scaglione. Egidilio. Is that Joey?"

"Yeah. He's in the VA Hospital in Pittsburgh. Stomach
trouble, I hear."

"Testa I know," Balzic said. "Anybody stopping in to see
his wife?"

"You got me. I think he had pretty good insurance though.
If she wasn't okay, you'd be hearing about it, as big a
mouth as she got."

"Let me see. That leaves Woznichak. Old Nick."

"Yeah, boy, was that awful. He didn't weigh a hundred
pounds. You didn't go to see him when he was laid out, did
you?"

"No. I didn't really like the guy that much."

"Christ, he looked like a shriveled-up baby in the casket."

"He was a big man all right. You know he was one of the
original Pittsburgh Steelers?"

"No, I didn't know that. I knew he played pro a long time
ago, but I didn't know that."

"Yeah. He was a real son of a bitch when he was young.
My old man used to tell me about him. Used to play the
game, go out and get bombed, and take on anybody that

looked crooked at him. Course he got his lunch, too. My old man told me one time he came in the Armenian Club, the one that used to be down behind Lockhart Steel. Remember, it used to be right across the street from the old police station?"

Stramsky nodded.

"Yeah, well, here comes this big guy, two-forty-something, drunk and running his mouth about he did this, that, and the other, and there's this little nigger sitting against the back wall. For some reason Woznichak really hated the coons, so he starts hollering at the little jig. My old man's taking it all in, not saying anything, but he knows the nigger. The guy shovels the coke furnaces all day six days a week and on Sundays he comes in the Armenian Club to get a load on and forget the shovel. Meantime, he doesn't know Woznichak from a bar stool, so he's definitely not impressed. Anyway, Woznichak goes over and says something like, 'I know Armenians are black, but you got to be the blackest Armenian I ever saw,' and the little jig, he doesn't say a word. He doesn't even get up. He just brings his foot up, and while Woznichak's going down, he lets him have it across the ear with the beer mug. One of those real heavy ones."

"I know the kind. You don't see them too much any more."

"Yeah. So Woznichak spends the next couple weeks in the hospital waiting for his nuts to quit looking like baseballs and telling everybody what he's going to do to the jig when he gets out."

"So what did he do?"

"Not a goddamn thing. He goes back to the club the Sunday after he gets out of the hospital and the joint is packed. Everybody's there. They all want to see him kill the jig. And the jig comes waltzing in at his usual time, orders his beer, and goes and sits where he usually sits. Woznichak starts hollering at him, but the jig says nothing. He just sits there drinking his beer until Woznichak starts for him. Then the jig stands up and lifts up his shirt and he says, 'You want to die, just keep coming.' He got a forty-five in his pants."

"It's a wonder he didn't get lynched."

"What's the wonder? Who was going to start?"

"Yeah, but still . . ."

"Still nothing. Who doesn't know how many big ones are in a forty-five?"

"Yeah, I guess."

"But the best part is Woznichak got to save a little something, so he offers to shake hands and forget the whole thing. The jig won't go for it, so then Woznichak says he wants to buy him a drink. The next thing you know, they're into a drinking contest, matching shots and beers, and Woznichak's paying, and the windup is, this little skinny jig drinks Woznichak flat—on Woznichak's money." Balzic thought a moment. "I don't know. It always tickles me to think about that. Even though the guy died bad—I mean, who'd wish cancer on anybody?—but that always tickles me to think he got his lunch that way. Hell, three ways." Balzic stood. "Well, that's it. There's nobody else you know of, right?"

"You got them all."

"Are all the farms listed in here too?"

"Yeah. In the back. There's copies of all the leases."

"Good enough. Hey. Where's Mary?"

"Up her mother's washing down the kitchen. I was supposed to help her. I'll catch hell for two days. . . ."

"Good luck on that," Balzic said. "See you tonight probably." He let himself out the kitchen door and made it down the walk and around the garbage cans to his car, driving back in the middle of quitting-time traffic. The day shift in South Rocksburg's mills was over.

Indian summer was hanging on. Balzic would have enjoyed it had he not stayed too long at Stramsky's and allowed himself to get caught in this line of cars and buses. He'd also drunk too much coffee and felt that he'd probably talked too much. He'd noticed a certain distance in Stramsky's eyes when he was telling that one about Woznichak. Had he told it before? He couldn't remember, but he probably had. He loved the story too much not to have told it before.

He tried to think where he should begin with the information he had. Minyon would have to be told. Balzic's mind focused on Minyon and then slipped quickly to thoughts of a cold bottle of beer, sweat streaming down its sides, a frosted glass . . .

He'd call Minyon. That was where he'd start. Give Minyon what he could use over the phone and then to hell with him. It was too hot, traffic was too bad, home and the refrigerator were too far away.

On the sidewalk, at the intersection by Grant's Five and Ten, there was a flash of tanned bare legs above sandals and below a short crimson skirt, and Balzic tried to catch sight of the face as the legs weaved through the clusters of straphangers waiting for the northbound buses. Then the legs were around the corner of Grant's and gone.

Ah, well, Balzic thought pleasantly, moving on when the light changed, the face might have been bad and then what. . . .

Balzic called Minyon from home and gave him the list of remaining farms leased by the club. He said nothing about the names.

"You're going to have to show me around," Minyon said.

"You've got people up there who know those farms as well as I do. Better maybe. Ralph Stallcup for one."

"Sergeant Stallcup was temporarily assigned to narcotics."

"Well, get him reassigned," Balzic said. "You're the chief of detectives."

There was a pause during which Balzic could hear the teletype. Then Minyon said, "That's right. I am."

Another pause. Balzic waited.

"I'm also in charge of this investigation," Minyon said, clipping off each word.

"There was never any doubt of that. So when are you bringing the dogs back?"

"I haven't decided that yet."

"Okay," Balzic said. "I'll be around if you want anything."

"I do want something."

"What?"

"Some names."

"Oh, I'm having them typed up," Balzic lied. "Should be up to you sometime tomorrow afternoon. Anything else?"

"Why can't I just have the membership rolls your man—what's his name? The Pol—the sergeant?"

"Stramsky. Because he's in the process of sending out bills and he needs the book."

There was another pause. "Wouldn't you say this was more important?"

"That's why I'm having the list typed up for you. Special." Balzic had to bite the inside of his cheek to keep from laughing. "Anything else?"

"Can't you get the list over here any sooner than that?"

"I'll do the best I can, Lieutenant. Is there anything else you can think of for me to do?"

"No," Minyon said, and hung up.

"Good-bye," Balzic said into the dead line. He hung up and was still laughing when Ruth walked into the kitchen from the back-yard patio.

"What's so funny?" she said.

"Ah, it's not as funny as it is pathetic," he said. "I was just pulling some monkey's chain. Just a couple short jerks to let him know somebody was on the other end."

"Whatever that means," Ruth said. "You ready to eat?"

"Let me take a shower first. Where is everybody?"

"Ma's on the patio taking a nap, and Marie and Emily are still at school. Aquatic club practice. You're home early."

"Feels like I been gone a month."

Balzic turned the car off North Main and headed north on Pine Hollow Road. The hollow was off to the right, hardly more than a deep gully, and if there ever had been any pines in it, they had long since been cut and sold as Christmas trees. Now it was a tangle of brambles and sumac trees with occasionally a locust tree breaking the monotony. The box numbers of the houses, all on the western side of the road as Balzic continued northward, grew smaller the farther he got away from town.

He found Peluzzi's house after backtracking twice and stopping at two other houses to ask directions. Peluzzi's mailbox, bearing neither name nor number, tilted precariously at roadside.

Balzic could not place the square, shabby bungalow in his memory. He recalled Stramsky saying that Peluzzi moved around, and he was sure then that Peluzzi had been living somewhere else when he'd been arrested the last time for assaulting his wife.

Balzic parked behind a recently polished maroon Pontiac, the car contrasting sharply with the bungalow, its white paint blistered and dirty, the yard a mass of ankle-high grass and pigweed. Balzic stumbled on a loose cinder block that served as a step from the berm to the yard.

Though perhaps an hour's daylight remained, lights shone out from both the windows facing the yard, but when Balzic knocked, one of the lights went off. He could hear a radio or a record player blaring and then being turned off.

Peluzzi answered the door in his underwear. He was carrying a towel, and his thick graying hair was wet. Balzic was surprised to see how short he was; somehow he remembered Peluzzi as being much taller.

"I don't want nothing, I don't need nothing," Peluzzi said, "so whatever you're hustling, go hustle it someplace else."

"Peluzzi?" Balzic said, producing his identification.

Peluzzi peered at the ID case and then at Balzic's face. "What the fuck do you want?"

"You remember me."

"How could I forget you? That mess cost me—never mind. What do you want?"

"I want to ask you some questions. Mind if I come in?"

"Do I have a choice?"

"Yes."

Peluzzi searched Balzic's face a moment, then stepped back out of the doorway. Balzic understood then why he'd had the impression that Peluzzi was much taller: he was thick through the neck, shoulders, and chest, and had long, heavily muscled arms.

"Lemme go put some pants on," Peluzzi said, and disappeared into the only room in the small house that seemed to have a door. The other three rooms—the living room, a room that must have been intended to be a dining room, and the kitchen—were connected by open archways.

Peluzzi returned wearing canary yellow slacks and carrying a pair of shined shoes and rolled-up socks. He sat on a wooden folding chair in what was supposed to be the dining room and put on the socks and shoes. There were five other chairs, none of which matched, and a round table that looked better suited to poker than to eating.

"Okay," Peluzzi said, picking up the towel he'd thrown on the table when he went to get his pants and wiping his hair, "so what's on your mind?"

"Where are you doing your hunting these days?"

"My what?"

"Your hunting."

"You come out here to ask me that?"

"I have a reason."

"I bet you do."

"Well?" Balzic said.

"I don't hunt too much any more."

"Why not?"

"Couple of reasons."

"Let's hear them."

Peluzzi wadded up the towel and tossed it into the kitchen. Then he bent down and retied one shoelace. "What the hell's this all about, Balzic?"

"Just give me the reasons."

"Okay. Number one, I ain't working. I missed three payments on that Pontiac out there and I had to sell most of my guns. I mean sixty bucks a week unemployment ain't exactly living. So how you supposed to hunt without a gun?"

"You sell them all?"

"Everything I could use around here. I still got my three thirty-eight Winchester, but that ain't exactly a squirrel gun."

"Sell your shotgun, too?"

"Gun? I didn't have *one*. I had three. I had a Winchester auto and a couple Italian jobs. A double over and under for skeet and a single for trap. I had to unload them all. I could've cried when I sold that trap gun. That mother cost me close to six bills, and all I could get for it was three bills."

"When was the last time you went hunting? I mean, you don't belong to the Police Rod and Gun Club any more."

Peluzzi laughed. "Is that what this is about—a membership drive? Or do I owe you bastards something too?"

"No."

"Well what then, Balzic? What's with all the questions? I got a date, man."

"A date?"

"Yeah. A date. What's wrong with that? I'm supposed to dry up and blow away or something? So I'm forty-six. I ain't dead yet for crissake."

"Somehow it just sounded, uh, never mind."

"Sounded how? Funny? So have a big laugh. My pleasure."

"When was the last time you hunted on club farms, Peluzzi—let's get back to that."

Peluzzi thought a moment, chewing his lip. "Season before last."

"Why did you quit?"

"Some guy told me about a preserve up around Indiana. Shoot as many pheasants as you want. Guaranteed. Good dogs and everything. Cost a helluva lot but it was worth it."

"Which guy? Gallic?"

Peluzzi's face lost its color. It lasted only a second, and then he regained both color and composure. But he stood abruptly and went into the kitchen. Balzic could hear the refrigerator opening and then a bottle being popped open. Peluzzi reappeared with a bottle of beer and stood in the doorway and drank from the bottle.

"Yeah, it was Gallic," Peluzzi said. "So?"

"He was a pretty good friend of yours, wasn't he?"

"We bummed around together, yeah."

"You did a lot more than bumming around. You went to Alaska with him. More than once."

"If you know, how come you're asking?"

"Whose idea was that?"

"Whose idea was what?"

"Whose idea was it to go on those trips?"

"What do you mean, whose idea? It was all our idea."

"All whose?"

"Mine. Gallic's, Richie Janeski's."

"How many trips did you make?"

"Where?"

"Anywhere. How many trips did you three make together?"

"I still wish the fuck you'd tell me what this is about."

"Just answer what I asked you."

"Why? I don't have to. You said when you came in I had a choice."

"You do. You can answer here or down at the station."

Peluzzi's eyes narrowed. Like the moment when his face had gone white at the mention of Gallic's name, the squint lasted only an instant, but it was intense and unmistakable. He turned sideways and let out a deep belch.

"You know, Balzic," Peluzzi said, facing Balzic again, "I can remember you from Mother of Sorrows?"

"You can?"

"Yeah. I only lasted till the second grade up there, and

then my old man couldn't go the freight no more. But I remember you. I was in second grade and you were in first. You were a nosy prick even then. You used to come around asking everybody what they had for lunch."

"I guess I'm just naturally inquisitive. Now which is it going to be—here or at the station?"

Peluzzi took another gulp of beer. "So what was the question? I forget."

"How many trips did you three make?"

"I don't know how many Gallic made by himself or with other guys. But me, him, and Janeski, we went to Alaska twice. Then we went up to Ontario fishing a couple times. Once we went fishing up in Manitoba. Then another time we went hunting in Mexico."

"You planning anything this year?"

"No."

Balzic studied Peluzzi's face. "Why not?"

"I told you, man. I'm busted out. I'm lucky I can go down Main Street. They're going to repossess my car for crissake. How am I going anyplace?"

"Is that the only reason?"

"What's that supposed to mean?"

"I mean, well, you three still buddies?"

"No." Peluzzi's eyes clouded over and then went wide. Again, he regained his composure quickly.

"What happened?"

"What happened—nothing happened! You buddy up with some guys for a while and then you don't. Nothing happened."

"You sure?"

"Aw, what is this? Sure I'm sure. I just don't see those guys no more. I don't know what for. Maybe we all got tired of hearing the same stories. Who knows?"

"When was the last time you saw them?"

"Summer before last. We went fishing up at Tionesta. Then I went hunting with Janeski couple of times. And that was it."

"You haven't seen them since? Neither one?"

Peluzzi shook his head.

"Isn't that a little strange? I mean, you three guys were pretty tight from what I hear."

"From what you hear. So what else do you hear? Come on, Balzic, cut the shit. What's this about?"

"I'll tell you the truth, Peluzzi, but you're not going to believe me."

"So give it a shot."

"I really don't know."

"You don't know! So what are you doing jerking me off like this? Jeeeezus Keeerist . . ."

Balzic turned for the door. "Listen, Peluzzi, I can't stop you from going anywhere, but just in case you should get a job in Cleveland or someplace, you be sure and let me know. I mean, right now I don't know what I'm doing, but pretty soon I might, understand, and if I do, I'll want to know where you are. Understand?"

"Yeah, yeah, I understand. You and my ex-wife's lawyer. Shit."

"See you around," Balzic said, and stepped outside. He was almost to his car when he heard the bottle smash against the wall, and he got in his car wondering how Peluzzi had managed to restrain himself for as long as he had.

It was shortly after eight when Balzic turned up Church Street in search of Rear 214. The street—named after Rocksburg's first superintendent of schools—began on North Main and led up a 10 per cent grade to a low-income housing project built by the government shortly after World War Two. Two blocks from the crest, Balzic spotted the number on a two-storied building, its exterior covered with imitation brick, a building, like the others on the street, which seemed to cling to its foundation out of spite for gravity.

Balzic turned the wheel to set the tires against the curb and got out, going to the rear of the building on a walk of flagstones between 214 and 216. Creaking wooden steps led up to a porch, and, at the top, Balzic took a guess and knocked on the first door he came to.

A pan-faced woman, her head mushrooming with plastic curlers, opened the door with an uncooked frankfurter in one hand and a large pickle in the other.

Balzic showed his ID and said, "I'm looking for a Richard Janeski."

"Next door," the woman said. "But I can tell you right now he ain't there."

"Do you happen to know where he is?"

"At work."

"Do you happen to know when he gets off?"

"Twelve. Same as my old man. But he won't come home."

"Do you know why not?"

"Sure. After they quit, they'll be down at Pravik's Hotel. Him and my old man. And they won't be home till they're good and stiff."

"Thank you. Sorry to trouble you," Balzic said, going down the steps wondering what reason Janeski had for not coming back. The reason why the pan-faced woman's husband didn't come home until he was stiff was fairly clear.

Balzic sat in the car a minute, thinking. He didn't want to spend four hours waiting for Janeski to show up in Pravik's, and he didn't want to go home. At either place he knew he'd start into the beer, and the way he was feeling, a start would only lead to an end: in Pravik's he'd get bored drunk; at home he'd get listless drunk. He could afford neither. He had to see Janeski tonight and Gallic tomorrow morning if he hoped to find out as much as he could by himself and still have the list of names to Minyon by tomorrow afternoon as he'd said he would.

There was no place else left. He turned the car around and headed it for the station.

He walked in, thinking he might talk Stramsky into some gin at a penny a point. Thinking that, he was unprepared for the Reverend Callum, who was pacing, head down and hands in his pockets, in front of the counter.

"You're a difficult man to locate," Reverend Callum said.

"I guess I am. Did we, uh, have an appointment?"

"No. As a matter of fact, we didn't. But I've been here twice today."

"Oh? What for?"

"I want to settle some of these things. The things I've been trying to settle for six weeks now. The things I brought up in council meeting."

"Let's go back here," Balzic said, nodding to Stramsky in passing and leading Reverend Callum to one of the interrogation cubicles in the rear of the squad room. He directed the reverend to a chair and took one himself. "Well," he said, "so what's on your mind?"

"This is not going to be easy for me to say," Reverend Callum said.

Balzic could see that it wasn't: the reverend couldn't stop rubbing his palms together and he was having a hard time looking at Balzic.

"I guess the only way to say it is to say it," Reverend Callum said. "I've been doing a little detective work of my own, and, well, I'm more than a little ashamed to say that I may have been seeing things that weren't there."

"Oh, listen, Reverend, if that's the way it is, just forget it. Those guys you were talking about, guys like Dawson and Williams, hell, they fool a lot of people. That's how they survive. That's their trade."

"I know that now, but in my first discussions with them, they seemed so sincere. And Williams's mother—now explain to me why she would go to such lengths to corroborate his stories after he'd beaten her. That's what I can't understand. It just doesn't make sense."

"Well, Reverend, I think what you mean is it shouldn't ought to make sense. Sense would be her admitting what he was. But it doesn't work that way. I'll tell you, I've been dealing with people like Williams—liars, bullies, mean, spiteful guys—I don't know, must be close to twenty-five years now. And you get a bully in here, a real mean kid like this Williams, and you won't find one mother out of a thousand who's going to say, 'Yeah, he's a no good sonuvabitch.' Excuse my language, Reverend, but, well, what do those words mean? I mean, what mother is going to say that about her son, no matter what words she uses? 'Cause you know what she'll be saying."

"Even after he beat her? And threatened to do worse?"

"Not even, Reverend. Because. Oh, they'll come in and make the complaint and they'll be raising all kinds of noise for a while about their kid, but then—well, take Williams and his mother. You know what happened after we arrested him that time—the time you were talking about?"

Reverend Callum shook his head.

"She went through everything, the complaint, the arraignment, the grand jury, but when it came to trial, she'd had some time to think about it. So when she gets on the stand, she refuses to say anything. She got on that stand and she wouldn't say anything except who she was and where she lived. She wouldn't even answer the question whether the defendant was her son or not. The trial lasted something like ten or twelve minutes. The judge threw it out. He had to. The stepsister wouldn't testify either."

"But why? I don't understand that."

"Aw come on, Reverend. They were scared. The worst kind of scared. That woman was scared of her own blood. She went through labor to have that kid. You think she's going to admit to the world—to herself—that she went through labor to produce a rat? Some women, they can do it. They can turn their back. They're not exactly rare, but they'd make a pretty small crowd. The rest, the Mrs. Williamses, well . . ."

"But surely the stepsister should have had other feelings. He wasn't her son."

"Yeah, but you got to remember what he'd already done to her. You ask any lawyer or any judge, they'll tell you, rape is one of the toughest cases to try. It's tough as hell to prove and it's just as tough to defend against."

"But he wasn't being tried for that. She'd dropped that charge."

"That's right. But the fact is she dropped it after we picked him up for assaulting her. Now you couldn't go to court with this, but the fact that she'd dropped it after he'd worked her over only proves to me that he had raped her. And I'll tell you what, a woman that's been raped—unless she's some kind of masochist—well, you give her time to think about it, she just don't want to have anything to do with the guy that raped her. Hell, most rapes, most real rapes, don't even get reported. 'Cause the victims just don't want to ever see that guy again. Now as far as the step-sister goes, she has that on her mind, plus she *has* to look at the guy all the time. He's around. And not just around, Reverend, but he's around working her over. I'll tell you straight. The only thing that's surprised me about the whole thing is the fact that she hasn't tried to kill him. Of course, nobody knows that she hasn't tried. Maybe that's what started him in on her the night we picked him up. Maybe she tried and missed. So, to make a long story short, Reverend, that poor female has got a hundred things going through her head, none of them easy to live with, and it's no wonder at all that she didn't testify against him. I don't think she could even if she wanted to. She could kill him a lot easier than she could talk about him to strangers."

Reverend Callum shook his head again. "I suppose I should apologize."

"Nah. No way. Forget it. What the heck, you make a mistake, that's all."

"So I did." The reverend straightened in his chair. "Have you, uh, checked into the other case I mentioned?"

"The Bivins kid? Was that his name?"

"That's the one."

"No, I haven't. I've had something else on my mind. Give me a minute and I'll get his file." Balzic left the cubicle and went to the live file next to the teletype. He motioned to

Stramsky to come over and asked him, "The name Bivins ring any bells, Vic?"

"Huh-uh. What's the preacher man bitching about—police brutality?"

"Something like that. He got some bad information, though."

"Wait a minute," Stramsky said. "You passed it. Back up a couple."

Balzic flipped the folders back and came up with the one bearing the name: "Bivins, Roland M." He opened it and scanned it quickly.

"Look at this. Arrested October 2, twenty-three forty-seven hours. Romeo's Lunch and Diner. Making threats and using abusive and obscene language. Arresting officer, Lawrence Fischetti." He turned to Stramsky. "Where the hell's the rest of it? Didn't he book him or what?"

"Beats the hell out of me," Stramsky said.

"Fischetti on tonight?"

"Huh-uh."

"Well call him, will you? I want to know what this is about. And tell him I don't want to hear any bullshit either. Christ almighty, he doesn't even have down here who made the complaint."

Balzic returned the folder to the file and went back to the cubicle where Reverend Callum was staring at his hands.

"How about some coffee, Reverend? Can I get you a cup?"

"No, thanks. I don't drink it."

"Ah, well," Balzic said, lighting a cigarette, "I think you may have a beef, Reverend. I'm not saying for sure, understand, but I've read Bivins's file and there are a couple of things out of sorts. Only thing is, the arresting officer isn't on duty tonight, so it may take a while."

"Are you trying to tell me that you'll call me?"

Balzic felt himself flush. "Listen, I give you my word. As soon as I know something, I'll let you know."

"What can I say?" the reverend said, standing. He extended his hand.

Balzic shook it and said, "As soon as I know, you'll know."

"That's all I can ask for," Reverend Callum said, and walked quickly through the squad room and was gone.

Balzic watched him go and then turned to Stramsky. "You get Fischetti?"

"His mother says he went out. She doesn't know where."

"Went out," Balzic said. "Shit. He doesn't come up with something good about this, he will be going out. And I'll be the one holding the door."

Balzic looked at the clock behind the bar and checked it with his watch. Three after midnight. He'd been in Pravik's Hotel long enough to have one draught and to order the second. He did not recognize the bartender and was trying to place him when the bartender returned with the second beer. Balzic asked if old man Pravik was still around.

"He's around all right," the bartender said. "Just barely. He had a stroke three weeks ago. Why? You a friend of his?"

"I know him," Balzic said, "but we're not friends. So who's taken over the place?"

"Me. For the time being." The bartender didn't seem at all pleased about it.

"You a member of the family?"

The bartender looked suspiciously at Balzic. "Yeah," he said. "I'm his son-in-law. One of them anyway. Why?"

"Just curious. I like to know who owns things."

"You with the Liquor Control Board?"

"No. I'm chief of police here."

The bartender thought about that. "Something wrong? I mean, I never saw you in here before."

"Nothing's wrong here. I'm just waiting for somebody I've been told comes in here pretty regularly. Name's Janeski. He works second trick at the can factory. You know him?"

"I haven't been here long enough to know last names. I'm from Farrell. Only other time I've been here was when I got married. The wife said we had to get married here. So we did, but except for then and now, I don't know anybody."

"What do you do up there? I mean, how are you able to take off and come down here and run this place?"

"That's a good question. Maybe you should come over to the old man's house and ask the rest of the relatives. They don't seem to understand when I ask them."

"Well, you must have a bar up there, right?"

"Right. So they just naturally think who better than me to run this one. In the meantime, I'm getting robbed blind up there, and they're sitting around waiting for the old man to die so they can divvy up this place. A real bunch of sweethearts, and what kills me is they don't think anything at all about it. My place, I mean. Christ, I'll be lucky the stools are still there when I get back." The bartender shook his head.

The door opened then and a group of six or seven men came in.

"Here comes a bunch from the can factory," the bartender said. "What was that guy's first name? Maybe I'll know him by that."

"Richard—Richie."

"Oh yeah. That's him. The one in the T-shirt with all the muscles and the messed-up face." He walked down the bar to wait on them.

Balzic didn't recognize any of them. Though the night had been chilly enough for Balzic to feel comfortable with a raincoat over his suit, all of them were in short-sleeved shirts or T-shirts. It was plain from their hands, wrists, and forearms they all were used to heavy labor.

Balzic watched them a minute or so. Four of them, after getting their beers, immediately began to play the bowling machine. A couple others settled into an argument begun elsewhere about the merits of players the Pittsburgh Steelers had traded away in recent years. The one identified by the bartender as Janeski sat by himself at the bar and took a newspaper from his back pocket and started to read it. He had the neck, shoulders, torso, and arms of a man who had spent years lifting weights.

Balzic went over to him with his ID cupped in his hand. "Janeski?"

"Yeah," Janeski said without looking up from the paper. Then he caught sight of the ID case Balzic held out, shielded from anybody else who might have been looking.

"I'd like to talk to you," Balzic said. "How about if we go sit in the back booth?"

Janeski hesitated, then folded his paper and jammed it into his back pocket. He swept up his glass of beer and followed Balzic to the booth. "So what do you want to talk about?" he said.

"I want to talk about your hunting."

"My what?" Janeski's nose had been broken and his mouth had been cut, probably a long time ago, but it had been bad when it happened. The scar of the cut was very wide, beginning on his left nostril and running diagonally across both lips and ending at the right side of his chin. It made him appear to be constantly sneering. Even his smile now at Balzic's question had what seemed a contemptuous twist to it. The injury had also left him with a slight lisp.

"Your hunting. Where are you going hunting these days?"

"Tell you the truth, I don't do much hunting any more."

"Any particular reason?"

"No time. I been working a lot of overtime. Can't get off."

"You used to hunt pretty regular with a couple guys, didn't you? Peluzzi and Gallic?"

Janeski took his time answering. "I used to hunt pretty regular, period."

"You seen those two lately?"

"What were their names again?"

"Peluzzi. Wheels, they call him. And Frank Gallic."

"Oh yeah, I used to hunt with them. Sure."

"You also belonged to the Police Rod and Gun Club."

"That's right."

"Why'd you quit the club?"

"I don't know if I had any special reason. I just quit."

"Wasn't it because Gallic talked you two, you and Peluzzi, into going to a preserve up around Indiana?"

"That might've been it. I don't remember now."

Janeski's gaze was steady, but his replies were as much questions as answers, and Balzic knew that he was going to have to pull everything out of him. The curious thing to Balzic, curious and suddenly absurd, was that he didn't know exactly what it was he was trying to pull out. First Peluzzi and now Janeski were both very much alive. What more could he learn? Still, the fact that both Peluzzi and Janeski had quit the club soon after somebody had been killed and scattered over club farms seemed to be reason enough to go on questioning Janeski. Nonetheless, Balzic had to admit that the matter of time could be pure co-incidence.

"When was the last time you saw either of them?"

"Who?"

"Come on, Janeski. Who've we been talking about?"

"Peluzzi and Gallic you mean? Oh, it's been a while."

"How long a while?"

"I don't know. Year maybe. Maybe longer."

"Didn't you go hunting with Peluzzi last year? And didn't the three of you go fishing—I think Peluzzi said something about going fishing up around Tionesta."

"Well, I remember going hunting with Peluzzi couple times. But I don't remember being on no fishing trip with them."

"Never? Or just the one at Tionesta?"

"Oh, we went fishing together. Up in Canada. Three or four times. I just don't remember this time you're talking about. At Tionesta."

"Peluzzi says you were there."

"Yeah? Well if he says it, maybe I was, and maybe I just don't remember it. Maybe I didn't catch anything."

Balzic's glass was empty, and Janeski's nearly so. "You, uh, ready for another one?" Balzic asked.

"You buying?"

"You go get them, I'll pay for them."

"Can't beat that," Janeski said, picking up the glasses and going to the bar. When he returned he said, with a lopsided grin, "Isn't every day the chief of police buys you a beer."

"My pleasure. Now to get back to this other thing—tell me again the last time you saw Gallic."

Again Janeski took his time answering. "A long time. I don't know."

"You think maybe it was that fishing trip to Tionesta?"

"Maybe. But I can't even remember being there. But if Peluzzi says so, maybe that was the last time."

"You didn't go hunting with him last fall? Not even once?"

"If I did, I can't remember." Janeski's tone had grown sharper.

"But wasn't it a fact that he's the one who talked you and Peluzzi into going up to that preserve?"

"I don't know if I'd call that a fact. He might've told us about it. Yeah, he probably did."

"Two people say he did. Peluzzi's one and Vic Stramsky's the other. Vic said that was the reason you gave him for quitting the club."

"Well, if he says it, it must be true, right? I mean, he's a cop, isn't he? A sergeant, too, if I remember right."

"What is it with you, Janeski? Why all the reluctance to talk about this?"

"Talk about what?"

"Come off it. You know what I mean?"

"Look, man. I just walked in here to get the taste of that mill out of my throat, and you start asking me all these questions. I don't even know what you're talking about. You haven't said a word yet about what this is all about. I keep waiting, but you just keep asking questions. But I'll tell you what it sounds like to me. It sounds like you think you know a lot of answers, so what I'm thinking is, if you know, man, what are you asking for?"

"I'm trying to put some things together, that's all."

"Oh, that's a good reason. That's a real good reason. I mean, now I understand everything." Janeski was sneering this time. There was no mistaking the effort from the perpetual sneer caused by the scar, and his face took on an even more ugly mien.

Balzic studied him a moment. He didn't know what he was going to say next; the idea suddenly occurred to him. "What happened that time you three were at Tionesta together?"

Janeski had been sloshing the beer around in his glass, watching the foam arc up to the rim. At Balzic's question he became suddenly quite still. His gaze remained fixed on the beer, but he seemed to be making a considerable effort to control himself. "I told you, man, I can hardly remember even being there, never mind what happened."

"A little while ago, you said you couldn't remember being there at all. Now you say you can hardly remember, but you can't remember what happened. I think you're lying."

Janeski's head swung up. "How do you know? You know so fucking much—how do you know what I remember and what I don't?"

"I know when somebody's trying to hide something."

"Yeah? So what do I have to hide, man? You tell me. I mean, you getting ready to arrest me or something? 'Cause if you are, man, you better tell me what for, and if it's for something that is supposed to've happened on this fishing trip, why don't you just tell me what it was? 'Cause I'd like to know."

"I don't know what happened. That's why I'm asking. I just know—"

"What?" Janeski said, his voice breaking. "What do you know?" He stood up, bumping the table with his legs and nearly spilling the beer. "I'll tell you what I know, man. I know I don't have to talk to you. I don't have to tell you a goddamn thing. I didn't do anything, so don't bother me no more. I don't have to tell you shit. You want to know what happened? Then you go back and talk to Peluzzi some more. Better yet, go talk to Gallic. Ask him to tell you what happened, that . . ." Janeski hurried to the bar, banged his glass down on it, and pushed his way through the group playing the bowling machine to the door and out.

Balzic sat there a moment rubbing his mouth. He'd struck a nerve, there was no doubt of that. But which nerve? And what was Janeski going to call Gallic—that what? The way Janeski had fought back the urge to call Gallic that name—whatever it was—convinced Balzic that something had happened among those three. But what of it? What did anything that happened among them have to do with anything? So there had been a falling out among cronies, an argument, a fight even. Suppose it was something more; suppose that—what did it have to do with those bones?

He left Pravik's then, telling himself that maybe Gallic would be more co-operative. But if Gallic wasn't? What if Gallic reacted the same way as Peluzzi and Janeski? But what difference would it make how any of them reacted? What did their reactions—no matter what they were—have to do with the bones?

Had there been somebody else with them, somebody whose name wasn't on the list of membership, somebody who wasn't even from around Rocksburg? And had they had their falling out over that somebody? Or had they had it with that somebody? Maybe the friends who thought they'd always been friends had turned out to be something other than friends?

Hell, Balzic thought, what am I trying to make out of two guys getting steamed about a fishing trip? Suppose they had gotten into a fight, suppose they had killed somebody—what possible reason could they have had for bringing the body all the way back here to take it apart and bury? Tionesta was over a hundred miles away.

If I had any sense, Balzic thought, getting into his car,

I'd dump this whole mess right in Minyon's lap. That was what Minyon wanted anyway, and he'd be doing himself a bigger favor than he would Minyon.

If it hadn't been for that damn dog of his, Balzic thought. "Bitch," he said. "Stupid, fat, contrary bitch . . ."

Balzic slept fitfully at best. Twice his mother, flushing the toilet, woke him, the first time at three and the second at six. The second time he tossed about for some minutes and then, fearing that his tossing would wake Ruth, he got up and went out into the kitchen.

He put water in a pan on the gas, and, while searching through the spice jars and cans for the instant coffee, the thought came to him as though he'd never slept: that fishing trip; Peluzzi, Janeski, and Gallic fishing the Allegheny River around Tionesta . . .

Something had happened: Peluzzi's face losing its color when he'd heard Gallic's name; Janeski first claiming not to remember even being there and then storming away in a barely controlled rage.

What name was Janeski going to call Gallic?

Balzic gulped two swallows of the coffee, dumping the rest in the sink and hurrying to the bathroom, there to lather himself under the shower and to shave, mindless of the strokes of the razor.

By seven o'clock he was at the station and by seven-thirty he had cleared up the routine matters. At a quarter to eight he was pulling off Route 331, seven miles out of Rocksburg, onto the gravel parking lot of Galsam's Freezer Meats.

It was a low, square building with the front right corner of it reserved for customer service, the facing of that portion all white tiles and large square windows. Scotch-taped onto the insides of the windows were signs painted in red and blue tempera on white butcher paper: "CHARGE ACCOUNTS WELCOME," "WE CUT FIRST, THEN WE WEIGH," "MASTER CHARGE HONORED," "ASK ABOUT OUR BAR-B-QUER'S SPECIAL," "DEER

HUNTERS, DEER SEASON WILL BE HERE BEFORE YOU KNOW—WE
CUSTOM SLAUGHTER DEER, $12.95 PLUS HIDE."

There was only one small light burning in the customer
service area. For some reason Balzic expected to see meat
cases, but there was only a Formica-covered counter ex-
tending the width of the room. A cash register sat in the
middle of the counter. Beyond the counter, he could make
out dimly two stainless-steel doors leading, no doubt, to
walk-in freezers. In the back wall on the right was a wooden
door.

As Balzic got out of his car and stepped around the side
of the building he could hear the soft mooing of cattle. The
smell came to him then, too.

Off to the right, about fifty yards away across a drive, a
large mobile home sat on a permanent foundation of cinder
blocks and mortar. Seventy-five to eighty yards behind that
one, beyond a weeping willow and a row of poplars and a
pair of short, thickly branched evergreens, was another
mobile home. It, too, appeared to be on a permanent
foundation.

In front of the nearer mobile home was parked a double-
cab International pickup truck bearing the same sign on its
door as was across the front of the building. Beside the
building was a Ford truck fitted with a bed for hauling live-
stock. In the drive beside the second mobile home was a
sedan, but, because of the trees, Balzic could not make out
the model or year. Between the two mobile homes, sitting
on four jacks on the grass, was a camper designed, Balzic
guessed, to fit the pickup truck.

Lights had been on in the second mobile home since Balzic had arrived, and, as he stood now, listening to the cattle
and to what he thought was the Conemaugh River, lights
came on in the near trailer. He could make out a shadow,
just the top of somebody's head, moving around inside.
Then the shadow went out of sight, apparently into another
room.

Balzic lit a cigarette and went back to his car to wait.

At eight o'clock exactly, fluorescent lights came on in the customer service area, the wooden door opened, and Mike Samarra, wearing a starched white coat and carrying a clean apron, came into the room.

Though it had been years since Balzic had seen Samarra, he recognized him at once. Except for the gray hair above his ears, Samarra seemed not to have changed. He was a bull of a man, with very little neck and large, rounded shoulders and wrists thicker than an ordinary man's ankle. He moved about in the same firm, no-nonsense gait that struck Balzic as characteristic, even at this hour of the day. Even as a kid, Mickey Samarra had had little nonsense about him. Balzic remembered him delivering ice in the mornings before school when most of the other kids were still trying to figure out how to stay warm just a minute longer.

Samarra came to the front door and, without so much as a glance at Balzic's car, unlocked it, then returned to the counter, going through the levered door to the cash register. After unlocking the register, he appeared to Balzic to be filling the cash drawer with money taken from his pockets. Only after he'd done that did he pause and take note of the car in his lot.

Balzic got out of his car and went inside and crossed the small room to Samarra with his hand out. "Mike, how are you? Remember me?"

"Mario?" Samarra's face twisted into a puzzled frown and then broke into a broad grin. "Mario Balzic. I'll be a son of a gun."

"You remembered. How about that. How are you, Mike?"

Balzic shook Samarra's hand, a hand with black hair like wires on the backs of the fingers. Though Balzic was more than a head taller, his hand was lost in Samarra's.

"I'll be darned," Samarra said. "Jeez, it must be ten years since I saw you."

"Yeah. Pretty long time, Mickey."

"Ha. I'll be darned. You know how long it's been since anybody called me that—Mickey? Son of a gun." Samarra grinned again. "Well, heck, what brings you out here? You looking for a good buy? Believe me, I've got them. I've got some terrific beef back here, Mario. Been hanging for almost six weeks. A guy was supposed to pick it up last week and he called yesterday and said he's leaving town or something. It's just right."

"Well, I'll tell you, Mickey, what I'm really here for is to see your partner."

"My partner?" Samarra's grin faded into an incredulous frown. His eyes began to dart about.

"Yeah. Gallic."

"Oh, Mario, you want to see him. I want to see him. Tina wants to see him." Samarra's voice was on the edge of despair.

"Tina?"

"Tina's my sister, Mario. Don't you remember? No, I guess maybe you wouldn't. She's a lot younger than us. She's twelve, no, thirteen, years younger. She'll be thirty-four the tenth of next month."

"Ah, just what do you mean you want to see him?" Balzic said.

"Just what I said, Mario. I haven't seen Frank for—wait a second. I'll tell you exactly." Mickey reached under his white coat and pulled out a wallet bulging with papers and cards. He took out a paper smudged with the color of the wallet. "Here it is. He went fishing on Friday, twenty-sixth of July a year ago. He came back the following Sunday night, and that was the last I ever seen him."

"I'll be damned," Balzic said. "I'll be damned."

"Mario, do you know something? I mean, if you know anything about this, Jeez, I hope to God you're going to tell me."

"Mickey, you forget. I came here looking for him, remember?"

"Oh. That's right." Mickey's face screwed up in thought. "But why? Why'd you come out here looking for him?"

Balzic picked his words carefully. "Oh, I just wanted to

ask him some questions. Had to do with the Rod and Gun Club. Our treasurer got his records fouled up and said Gallic would know what he needed to know. I wasn't doing anything, so I said I'd come out and find out for him."

"Oh," Samarra said, and Balzic knew he'd accepted the explanation. "Mario," Mickey said suddenly, his words coming in a rush, "I tell you, it's the darndest thing. I knew that guy since 1942. I mean I knew him a little bit before when we were kids in school, but I really didn't know him, if you know what I mean, until we went into the Army. Then we got to know each other pretty good. You know, we sort of got thrown together. And you know how it is when you have to go away from home, all those strangers around, you don't know what's going on half the time. Anybody that's from your home town is like a cousin or something.

"Well, we went through everything together—training, we went through Africa, through Italy, the whole shooting match. And a lot of the times the thing that kept us going was what we were going to do when we got out. We were always making plans. You'd be surprised how much just making plans can keep you going. I'd've never believed it myself if somebody told me.

"Well, we did get out—God knows how. Without a scratch, neither one of us. And so we just naturally tried to do what we planned all those times. It just seemed like the thing to do. First, the grocery up in Norwood, then the butcher shop across from the old Mother of Sorrows grade school, and then, finally, this place. We went through hell together, Mario. All kinds of hell. But good times, too.

"But then one day—phffft—he takes off. Not a word. Not so much as a post card. Nothing. My God, Mario, we were together nearly twenty-seven years. Imagine! Jeez, I thought Frank was my best friend. It turns out I didn't know him at all. I can't get over it. If I could understand it, maybe —ah, what's the use talking?"

"Mickey, did he, uh, beat you out of anything?" Balzic said.

"No! That's the real puzzle. That's what I really can't understand. He didn't take a penny. Jeez, he didn't even take what was his. And he never has, either. I just called the bank again two days ago. Eleven thousand dollars, Mario. Still in his account! Mario, I tell you, it doesn't make sense. Heck, he didn't even take his truck."

"The pickup?"

"Yes. The camper, too. He left everything. My God, all his guns. You know, for a long time I thought maybe he drowned. He used to drink sometimes. Sometimes he drank way too much, but it didn't interfere with the work, so I never said anything about it. But, anyway, he used to fish sometimes at night, and I was always telling him to watch out. The river's shallow back there, but it's pretty fast. You go off those rocks, you're gone. You know, I hired three—what do you call them?—scuba divers? Yeah. I paid them out of my own money, not out of the business money. I had them for a week. My God, I don't know how far down the river they went, but they didn't find a thing. Nothing."

"Mickey, why in the hell didn't you call us?"

"The police? Mario, I know you'll think I'm crazy, but when you're in business, dealing with the public, boy, I'll tell you, people are funny. They think something's wrong, boy, they stay away. And the police, well . . ."

"Yeah, I know. The police always mean something's wrong."

"That's right. Even if nothing's wrong, your customers will think there is and, boy, once they go away, they don't come back."

"You still should've called us, Mickey. Me, anyway. I'd have kept it quiet."

"Ah, Mario, I didn't know what to do. I'll tell you who I did call, though. I called the Missing Persons. About a month after. Right after I had those divers come in. And I asked them to please keep it quiet—which they do anyway,

I found out—but they never came up with anything. Nothing. I just called them again last week. It's like—Mario, I'll tell you. It's like Frank was never even here. And my God, Tina—she was, they were supposed to get married. Tina, boy, I wish I knew what to do for her."

"Is that who lives in the front trailer?"

"Yeah. That used to be Frank's. I have the one in back. Tina, my God, Mario, she just mopes around, don't say anything, won't talk to the customers. I don't know what to do with her. I mean, sure, it's a real blow, but to me, too. Not just to her. But I guess it's not the same."

"How tough is it on you?"

"Mario, are you kidding? Never mind the work, I'm going nuts trying to keep the figures straight. The taxes. My God. And then we were having trouble with a new inspector. I knew he was a grafter the second I seen him. He wanted something in the back pocket just to give us the same rating we always had."

"When was this?"

"A year ago last April. We had troubles back and forth with the federal people, and everything was just about to get cleared up when Frank leaves. Now it's still hanging fire. Frank could deal with those people. I mean, that was what he was really good at. He could really talk. But with me, those guys start throwing those legal words around, I'm like a clown. Mario, I tell you, I don't know whether I'm coming or going sometimes."

"What's the problem with the taxes?"

"Oh, God," Samarra said, throwing up his hands. "We pay taxes to everybody. The city, the county, the state, Washington. We pay quarterly, you know. All along, right from the beginning we made a rule both of us would sign the checks. Everything except personal income tax. And ever since he's been gone, well, I've been signing everything. I've even been paying his income tax."

"What the hell for? He's not around."

"I—I don't know. I just want everything to look right. Just in case."

"Just in case what?"

"Well, I mean, in case he comes back."

"Hell, Mickey, his taxes would be something he'd have to settle."

"Yeah, but what if—I mean, the government's tough, Jeez. You screw up with the Internal Revenue, I could go to jail."

"Oh, come on, Mickey. Anybody else wouldn't even think twice about it. Hell, half the country is trying to beat Uncle out of every cent they can, and you're paying double. What's your layyer say about all this?"

"I don't have a lawyer. We never needed one. We didn't cheat."

"God, Mickey, I don't know how you do it. My advice to you—get a lawyer, man. Put your mind at ease about these things. I'm no expert on tax law—hell, I have to go to H. & R. Block myself, that's how dumb I am about it, but I can't believe that you'd have to pay income taxes for a partner that isn't there. Not even Uncle's that greedy. Tell you what. How about I call up Mo Valcanas and make an appointment for you?"

"Isn't he the criminal lawyer?"

"He does everything."

"But I'm not a criminal."

"Forget that, will you? Listen, if nothing else, what happens if Gallic never shows up? No matter how legal you've been, no matter how straight you tried to keep everything, you've still got problems. You need somebody to advise you about these things."

Samarra hung his head. For a second Balzic thought he was going to break down. Then his head came up and he looked squarely at Balzic. "I'd appreciate it, Mario, if you'd get this Valcanas for me, but what I want you to know—honest to God—I haven't done anything wrong.

Everything I did, I did to keep the business going. I don't know. I wanted it right when Frank came back."

"You really think he's going to?"

Samarra sighed. "Oh, God, what do I know? I keep hoping, that's all. I mean, if he does, ah, what the heck do I know?" He put his hands on the counter and supported his bulk against his stiffened arms. "You know what I think, Mario? I mean what I really think?"

Balzic waited.

"I think something bad happened that weekend he went fishing, that's what I really think."

"What makes you think that?"

"Those two guys he went with. Ah, I don't know. I never liked them. And Frank, he was always going off somewhere with them. Canada, Alaska, Mexico. You know, this place used to be full of stuffed heads? My God, there used to be a polar bear right over there in that corner, and over there, in the other corner, there was a brown bear. A Kodiak. Huge things. That darn polar bear was almost nine feet high."

"What happened to them?"

"They're all in the back. All his stuff is. He must've had fifteen heads. Animals I don't even know the names of, never mind the deer heads and racks."

"Whose idea was that?"

"To put them in the back?"

Balzic nodded.

"Tina's. She made me. She said she couldn't stand to look at them no more. I thought it would help her. She thinks I threw them out, you know—gave them to the garbage men. That's what I told her, but I couldn't bring myself to do that. So I put them where she doesn't go. They're in the back of the big freezer. Both bears, everything. I got them covered up with dropcloths."

"Where is she now?"

"Over in the trailer. She's supposed to come over about eight-thirty, quarter to nine. But more and more she doesn't come over until she hears a customer's car. Even then, sometimes I have to call her on the intercom. I tell her, Tina, you got to quit moping around. You're young yet, you got to get out of here once in a while. She just looks at me. My God, yesterday she told me to shut up. The first time in my whole life she ever said that to me. She's my sister, Mario, but ever since our parents died, I been, well, you know, more than just a brother. And my God, it's breaking me apart to see her like she is now. It's like, God forbid, it's like she don't care whether she lives or not. God forgive me for saying that, but I never said it before. . . ."

"Mickey, uh, think a minute. You said you think something bad happened that weekend, right?"

Mickey nodded.

"But then you said Frank came back on the Sunday after he left, right?"

"Yeah."

"And the truck's his? The pickup?"

"That's right."

"Well, how could he have got back here if something happened during that weekend?"

"That's another thing I can't figure out. The truck is here, but Frank ain't."

"Do you mean you didn't see him? I mean actually see him? That Sunday night."

"No. Did I say that? No. I didn't see him. I just woke up Monday morning to start work and I saw the truck. Parked right where it is now."

"You mean it hasn't been moved?"

"Oh, no, no. It's been moved. Sure, I take it down to the gas station every once in a while to get the battery charged and keep air in the tires. And all last winter I used to start it up every day and run it awhile, you know. I made sure there was antifreeze in it. And I keep the inspections up to date. But I don't drive it around. It's Frank's."

"Does Tina?"

"Oh, God no. She won't go near it. I swear, I don't even think, I mean, this is going to sound funny. Sometimes I'm in here with a customer, and she'll be coming over from the trailer, and she has to walk right by the darn thing. She looks like she doesn't even know it's there. I can't explain what I mean. Do you get what I mean?"

Balzic nodded. "You think she'll be coming over pretty soon?"

"I don't think so. Lately, I don't know." Samarra hesitated. "Ah, what the heck. I may as well tell you. Yesterday when she told me to shut up, you know what that was about?"

Balzic waited.

Samarra pushed away from the counter and started to pace about, pulling and tugging at his thick fingers. "Those two guys, the ones Frank used to pal around with, well, I never liked them. They never did anything to me, understand. It's just that when Frank was with them, I'd know about it the next day. Sometimes for the next couple days."

"How do you mean?"

"I can't explain it too good, Mario. But he'd be different. Even when he'd just go around town drinking with them during the week. When he'd wake up, he wouldn't just be hung over. He'd, well, he wouldn't talk to me for a while. And then when he did, he wouldn't say no more than he absolutely had to. He'd act like I was the dumbest guy in the whole world. Now, you know me good enough from when we were kids, Mario. I mean I never was any brainstorm. But I know my work. I know how to get along with the customers. And I'll tell you, I kept the books in every business we had. Every one, and there never were any mistakes. Oh, the register might be off a couple bucks, but heck, that happens in any business no matter how close you watch it. But never anything big."

"I understand," Balzic said.

"Okay. So what was I starting to say?"

"About those two guys and Tina telling you to shut up."

"Yeah, that's it. Well, Frank was usually real nice to me most of the time. Not that we carried on any big conversa-

tions. Heck, you work together as long as we did, you don't
have to talk much. You know everything that has to be done.
But lots of times we'd be in the back working and we'd be
singing. Singing like crazy. I like to sing, you know. I been
singing in church since before my voice changed. And Frank
had a nice voice, too. He could only sing melody, but I'd
sing harmony, and it made the day go, too, you know? But
when he'd be out with those two, I don't know, two, three
days, sometimes a week would go by before he'd want to
sing again. And if I tried to start, he'd just give me this
look, like, why don't you dry up? You know—I mean, he
never said it right out, but you see what I mean?"

"I see. So what happened yesterday?"

"Well, yesterday, I don't know. I couldn't stand it. I was
thinking about the taxes, about everything, and I said to
myself, I got to talk to those two guys—"

"You never talked to them before?"

Mickey shook his head.

"Never? Not even once? In all this time?"

"Never. I told you, I didn't like those two. I knew Peluzzi
from way back. He ain't a good person, Mario. Never was.
I remember the way he used to talk to his father when he
was a kid. God, if I ever talked to my father like that—ah,
never mind. Anyway, I thought about it—calling them up—
and I thought and I thought. So, finally I decided to ask
Tina about it, to see, you know, if she thought it was a good
idea, and if she did, then I was going to do it."

"This was yesterday?"

"Right. I couldn't sleep the night before with thinking
about it. So when she comes in, I tell her what I'm thinking.
My God, I thought . . ."

"What?"

"I thought, wow, the way she looked at me. And did
she ever tell me off. Mind your own business, she says,
and what do you know, she says. She's not hollering or anything, but, boy, I know she's really mad. Then she says she
never wants to hear those two guys' names again. Never.

And I tried to interrupt her to tell her maybe they know something, and that's when she tells me shut up. My God, Mario, I could've cried right there."

"Is that what makes you think something happened that weekend?"

"Huh? I don't follow you."

"Well, I mean you said you were thinking that before Tina acted that way."

"Oh yeah. Sure."

"So what do you think now?"

"Now? I'll tell you. Now I'm convinced. I mean, ain't you?" Mickey continued to pace about, pulling and tugging at his fingers. "Mario, this'll maybe sound funny, but I'm really glad you came. My God, you don't know what a relief it is to talk to somebody else about this. I haven't been able to talk to anybody about it. It's all inside—Frank, Tina, the business. It's like I'm in a pressure cooker and something's wrong with the valve. I think sometimes I'm going to explode. My God, I didn't get two hours' sleep last night. And without the pills I wouldn't even get that much . . . but the thing that really convinced me, to get back to this thing I started to say, well, how did Frank get out of here? I mean, the truck's here. He never had a car. Always a truck. Used to get a new one every two years. So how'd he leave from here if it wasn't with those two guys?"

"Did you ever stop to think that he never came back?"

"What?"

"You said yourself you never saw him after he left that Friday, right?"

"My God, I never thought of that." Mickey stopped his pacing and clasped his fingers together on top of his head. "You see what a real smart guy I am."

"Course that wouldn't explain how the truck got here," Balzic said.

"Huh?"

"Nothing. I was just thinking out loud. Say, do you think I could go over to talk to Tina?"

"Huh? Oh no, you better not."

"Why not?"

"'Cause she told me never to come in there. And if she won't let me in there, Mario, well . . ."

"Uh, Mickey, how long's she been living there?"

"About three months. I'll tell you exactly." He reached into his pants again for the thick wallet. He found another scrap of paper. "Yeah. Here it is. She came back three months ago yesterday."

"Where was she living before that?"

"Well, you know, I held onto my parents' house in Norwood, and she lived there. Then about a month after Frank didn't come back, she said she had to get out of here. So I said—"

"Get out of here?" Balzic interrupted.

"Oh you know. Not out of that house. I mean here. Every place. She said this place was making her crazy. She said she couldn't stay around here any more. So I said, where you going to go? And she said she wanted to go to Theresey's for a while. In Toledo. Theresey's the oldest girl, Mario. You remember her."

"Yeah. I remember. She married Tony Ianni. Did she go? Tina?"

"Yeah. I drove her up. And she stayed there a year. Then, like I said, she came back. I didn't know she was coming. She just showed up here three months ago yesterday. I don't even know how she got here. She must've took a bus."

"And she moved right into the trailer?"

"Yeah."

"Didn't you think that was a little strange?"

"Tell you the truth, I did. But she was acting so funny for so long, I thought if that's going to make her feel any better, let her. The place was just sitting here. What could it hurt?"

"She ever in it before? I mean when Frank was here?"

"Oh yeah. Sure. I told you, they were getting ready to get married. She was in it lots of times."

"Mickey, don't get mad when I ask you this, okay?"

"Don't get mad about what?"

"Well, she's your sister. . . ."

"Go ahead, Mario. I won't get mad."

"She ever spend the night there?"

"Ah, Mario, none of us are kids. She was no kid either. What they did, I didn't think about. I didn't ask about it either. And what I saw, I pretended I didn't see. Besides, they were talking about marriage. Anyway, it was with Frank. It wasn't with some stranger, some guy she met someplace. I mean, until this, you know, I thought he was, ah, never mind what I thought."

"So she did spend some time with him?"

"Sure. What do you think? But I'll tell you what. I thought it would be good for them. Frank, he used to bring some real floozies home sometimes. I used to wonder where he found them. Real skags, you know? I never said anything to him, understand, but I'll tell you, there were times when I'd find myself praying a little bit that he wouldn't catch nothing. My God, there would've went our license. . . ."

"How long were they going together?"

"You know, Mario, it was real funny. Tina worked for us since the summers when she was in high school. And Frank, he never looked like he knew she was around, and then all of a sudden, it's like he can't think about anybody else. That was about three years ago. Then they were always together, I mean, except for the times when he was with Peluzzi and Janeski. Frank took her hunting, fishing. Heck, he even taught her how to dress game. That was real funny. She was around this business practically all her life, and she never once so much as asked how you do it. Then, deer season two years ago, she even helped out in the back, you know, when we got jammed up."

"She helping you now?"

"That's another funny thing. I asked her to help me, 'cause, you know, now I really need the help, but now she's like she was before. She don't go near the back. Otherwise, I wouldn't've felt free to put Frank's stuff back there."

"I see," Balzic said. "Well, listen, Mickey, I'll get in touch with that lawyer for you. I have to go now. But I'll be in touch, okay?"

"Mario, before you go, I mean, you been asking a lot of questions. What do you think?"

"Not much of anything right now," Balzic lied. "I just wish to hell you'd called me when Frank didn't show up. Fifteen months is a long time. But don't worry. I'll be thinking about it. And I'll keep in touch," he said, going out to his car.

He sat in the car for a few seconds, looking at the pickup and the trailer where Frank Gallic had once lived and where Tina Samarra was now living. "I'll be damned," he said, and then turned the car around and drove back along Route 331, heading into Rocksburg until he came to Five Point Intersection, there turning up Willow Creek Road to go the back way to the state police station.

He parked in the area reserved for people taking driving tests and went in through a back door, nodding to troopers he knew as he made his way into the duty room. A portly female typist Balzic didn't know was transcribing something from a recording machine; a trooper Balzic had seen once or twice was seated at the radio console directing extra mobile units to an accident; and Corporal Ed Bielski was talking to a citizen at the front counter.

Balzic stood by the counter and smoked until Bielski finished with the citizen.

"Mario," Bielski said, "how goes it?"

"It goes. Sideways, backwards, but it goes. Where's Minyon?"

"The lieutenant," Bielski said, "is hard at it, doing his duty behind a bunch of bloodhounds."

"He got fresh dogs in already? I'll bet the handlers liked that."

"Thrilled beyond belief. At least that's what I heard. I wasn't here."

"They got here before you came on?"

"An hour before I came on to be exact. And Lieutenant Minyon was waiting for them. He also had a certain sergeant with him. I think you know the man. Stallcup? Seems he was up and about at that hour because you recommended him to the lieutenant. Least that's what I hear."

"Stallcup pretty hot about it, huh?"

"I hear he wants to speak many words with you."

"What the hell," Balzic said. "It'll do him good to chase Minyon around the boonies. He's putting on a little grease."

"I'll tell him you said that," Bielski said. "So, Mario, what can I do for you?"

"I just want to borrow a typewriter for a while, that's all. I promised Minyon a list of names."

"Help yourself. You know where everything is. Anything else?"

"Yeah, there's one thing you could do, if you would. Call Rocksburg Savings and Loan. Tell them it's routine but confidential. Here's the names. Find out what these two got, what's been taken out and put in and approximate dates for, say, the last year and a half." Balzic wrote on a pad the names of Michael Samarra and Frank Gallic and pushed the pad around to Bielski.

"That's easy enough. Anything else?"

"Well, you might ask if they happen to know who these two carry insurance with. They might know, they might not. It's a long shot."

"Good enough. You know where the typewriters are."

"I'll find one," Balzic said, and set off through the maze of offices and cubicles to find a machine not in use. He located one after a minute or two and, using his index fingers, he pecked out the three names and addresses of Janeski, Peluzzi, and Gallic. When he'd finished, he won-

dered why he'd even bothered, just as he wondered why
Minyon was out with the dogs.

Minyon, of course, didn't know what he knew and so
would naturally be out looking for what he could find, trying in his own way to establish identity. Still, Balzic
couldn't help thinking it was a waste of time and energy:
a positive identification of the bones would only prove what
he already knew.

He walked back into the duty room as Bielski was hanging up the phone.

"What did you come up with, Ed?" Balzic asked.

"Couple of pretty rich guys, these two. This Samarra had
over twenty grand in his account. Twenty-one thousand,
one hundred and fifty-three bucks, give or take some
change. What the hell's he do?"

"He's a butcher. Just a dumb butcher. Nice guy, but
dumb."

"The other one, Gallic, he's not too bad off either. He's got
eleven thousand and four bucks and change. He a butcher
too?"

"He was."

"Regular deposits for Samarra," Bielski said, reading from
his notes, "but the other one hasn't made any deposits since
the June before last."

"Figures. How about withdrawals?"

"Every three months for both of them. The amount varies,
but never more than three hundred bucks."

"They say who made the withdrawals?"

"Apparently this Samarra."

"Also figures. They say anything about who they have
their insurance with?"

"Yeah. We got lucky there. Their agent just happens to
be one of the directors of the savings and loan."

"So?"

"Seems they're partners—"

"Yeah."

"—so they had a big fire, theft, storm, and liability policy on the business, a Galsam's something or other."

"Freezer Meats."

"Yeah, that's it. Anyway, it's all-inclusive and pretty big. This Samarra had life insurance, fifty thousand worth, with his sister, a Christina Marie Samarra, as beneficiary. The other one, Gallic, seems he didn't believe in it. Both of them had medical insurance which, in addition to covering all the usual expenses including major medical, also paid them fifteen bucks a day so long as they were unable to work. That's about it."

"It's about what I expected," Balzic said. "Thanks, Ed."

"Don't mention it. What have you got there?"

"This is the list Minyon wanted. Tell him it's here when he gets back."

"Is this about the bones?"

"Yeah."

"Just yeah? Nothing else? You don't want me to tell Minyon anything else?"

"Why? Do I look like I got something else to tell him?"

"I don't know, Mario. You sort of look like you know something."

"Oh, I know lots of things, Ed. Trouble is, none of them makes too goddamn much sense right now." Balzic headed for the back door. "Listen, Minyon wants me, tell him I'll be down my station until eleven or so, then I'll be out the club range until noon. Afterwards, back at the station until four-thirty or so and then home for a while. Okay?"

"Okay, Mario. He'll be asking. See you later."

Balzic went out to his car thinking that he'd hate to be in Bielski's place. Bielski had to have learned by now how Minyon felt about Polacks; Minyon wasn't nearly subtle enough to hide his prejudice, and Bielski wasn't due for a transfer for at least a year. If that wasn't enough, Bielski should have made sergeant six months ago, and it was common knowledge that he was smarting about his test result. Given those preconditions, Balzic wished he could observe

Bielski when Minyon returned: how much of what Bielski learned in the past half hour would he tell Minyon? how would he say it? would he say anything at all without being prodded? Poor Bielski, Balzic thought. The best he could hope for was an early transfer, and with luck, he'd get sent to Wilkes-Barre, to where Minyon had just come from.

Balzic pulled into the space reserved for him at city hall and went into the station just as Patrolman Larry Fischetti, in street clothes, was parking his car.

Desk Sergeant Angelo Clemente was busy at the radio. A mattress fire in somebody's attic was tying up traffic in The Bottoms, the section of Rocksburg on the flat by the Conemaugh River where a half dozen truck terminals and the larger mills and fabricating plants were located. From Clemente's face, Balzic could see what a mess it was, but he didn't interfere, proceeding instead to the live file. He rooted out the file on Roland Bivins and took it back to one of the interrogation cubicles, there to wait for Fischetti.

"Back here, Fish," Balzic called out.

Fischetti, in his early twenties, recently returned from Vietnam, a heavyweight wrestler in high school, came into the cubicle looking, Balzic thought, too intimidated for anybody's good.

"Sit down, Fish," Balzic said, pushing the Bivins file around so Fischetti could read it. "Okay, so explain this."

"I screwed up," Fischetti said, without looking at the file.

"Hey, goddammit, I ain't a priest. I don't want a confession. I want an explanation."

"I did everything wrong. I lost my head. The kid got me hot and I just forgot everything."

"More interpretation I don't want. Will you just tell me what happened?"

"Well, I was on my beat and I made my call in from the box and Stramsky tells me to check out a disturbance in the diner. Romeo's place. It's late. I'm getting ready to go off. I'm tired. I'd been out with my dogs all morning—"

"So?"

"—so anyway, I go in and there's this little fart hollering his head off. I can't make sense of what it's all about, but as soon as he sees me, he starts in on me. 'Here comes the pig,' he says. Now meanwhile, there are about four or five others in a booth, and I'm thinking, hell, man, watch yourself. You do this wrong, you could really screw things up. So I walk back to him, you know, easy, and I haven't said a word. I stop about three, four feet away from him, and I ask him what's going on. He says, 'None of your business, mother-fucker,' and he calls me a pig again, and I look at him and I think, Christ, he's just a kid. Can't be fifteen. Meanwhile Romeo is going nuts. He's hollering at me, the kid's holler-ing at me, the other spooks in the booth, they're laughing, and everybody else in the place—I don't know, I could just feel everybody watching me to see what I was going to do."

"So what did you do?"

"Chief, honest to God, I don't remember what I did. All I know is, the next thing I had him outside. I had a real good take-along on him. He couldn't move. Which was no big thing. I mean, I had him by forty pounds at least."

"And?"

"Well, he wouldn't shut up. He just kept calling me names, motherfucker and pig and honkie. I think I told him to shut up or he was going to get hurt."

"Beautiful," Balzic said. "So then what?"

"Well, I got him to the call box and I tried to call in for a mobile unit, but he's hollering at me so loud, cars are stop-ping and Stramsky can't hear what I'm saying and I'm get-ting hotter by the second. So the only way I can figure to get him to shut up is to make the take-along tighter. You know, put it on him so it hurts."

"And you did."

"Yeah. I put the phone down and I got a new grip. I really wanted to break his arm."

"What then?"

"I told him if he didn't shut up I would. Break his arm, I mean. And he did. The mobile got there, and I put him in and brought him down here."

"What time was that?"

"Well, it was after twenty-four hundred. I knew that because Stramsky was gone and Royer was on the desk."

"Then what?"

"Then I put him in the lockup."

"And?"

"That's when I really screwed up. I was shaking so bad, I just filled out the report half assed and I went home."

"Half assed is right. What did you tell Royer?"

"I don't even remember talking to Royer."

Balzic rubbed his mouth and sighed. "Christ . . ."

"Chief, I've been thinking about it ever since it happened. I was going to come and tell you about it every day, but I couldn't. . . . I think I ought to quit. I don't think I'm cut out for this."

"That's right," Balzic said, "add self-pity to it. That makes it perfect. Listen to this, goddammit, you're not quitting. But I'll tell you what you are going to do. You're going to explain this to a certain black preacher. And then you're going to spend some time talking to somebody else I know. Goddammit, there's no excuse for what you did. None. I mean I can understand taking the heat because a snot calls you names. That I can understand. But that doesn't mean you forget everything you know. This report is absolutely inexcusable. And Christ almighty, not bothering to arraign the kid—Jesus, Fish, what the hell were you thinking about? You don't even know what happened to the kid."

"Royer told me a couple days later he held him for a couple hours and then called his mother and let him go."

"Yeah. A couple days later you find out!" Balzic took out his notebook and wrote down two names. "Here. You call these two people and you arrange to see them. At their earliest convenience, you got that?"

"Yes, sir." Fischetti looked at the names. "Who are they?"

"That Callum is the black preacher. He's the one who brought this mess to my attention. I had to hear it from him in a city council meeting, for crissake. The other one, Higgins, is a psychologist."

"A what?" Fischetti looked deeply injured.

"You heard me right. A psychologist. He's a little, skinny, light-skinned spook. Maybe, if you pay attention, he'll teach you something about dealing with spooks. If nothing else, maybe he'll convince you they're just people, because right now I have the feeling you don't think so. And don't worry about paying him. That'll come out of department funds. But you're going to have to arrange your own transportation and you won't get reimbursed for that. He's in Pittsburgh. And I want to know by tomorrow—no later—that you arranged to see these guys. You hear me? No later than tomorrow."

"Yes, sir."

"All right. Now get out of here and do it. One more thing."

"What's that?"

"Forget about quitting, understand? 'Cause I won't let you."

"Yes, sir."

"And get your chin up off your chest, for crissake. Everybody fucks up once in a while."

"Yeah. Sure."

"Change your tone, goddammit. Everybody does fuck up once in a while. How do you think I feel? I didn't even know about this until last week, and then I had to stand there like a jerk and tell the whole damn council I didn't know anything about it. And you think that spook was calling you names? What the hell do you think they're calling me? And you know what? I rate a few of those names. Not all of them, understand. But a few."

"Yes, sir."

Balzic made as though he was going to punch Fischetti. Instead, he gave him a light slap and then pinched his cheek. "Get out of here now," he said. "Go have a beer and call those two guys. And learn something from this," he called out as Fischetti was heading for the door.

"What's the matter with the kid?" Clemente said.

"He's a kid, that's what's the matter with him. But keep your fingers crossed anyway, Angelo. If we're lucky, we won't get sued."

Driving out to the Rod and Gun Club rifle range, Balzic tried to empty his mind of all the questions crowding in and yammering to be answered. He succeeded as long as he was shooting. The demands of the Springfield 30.06, aiming, breathing, squeezing off the shots, took all his concentration. It was the primary reason he liked to shoot. As much as he was shooting to keep himself proficient and prepared, he fired his twenty rounds at the silhouette targets to forget whatever else was pressing in on him. It was impossible to shoot well and think about anything else.

The moment he bent down to pick up the last empty cartridge case, the questions started to form, and by the time he'd taken down the targets and rolled them, his mind was again a jangle.

Gallic. Frank Gallic . . .

The name kept rushing to the front of his mind, so that Balzic, without being aware of it, was saying the name aloud as he put the targets in the trunk of his car and slipped the Springfield into its case. He stood with his hand on the trunk lid and asked himself who Frank Gallic was.

As defined by Mickey Samarra, Frank Gallic was hardly more than a shadow. The words Mickey had used to describe him: "best friend," "used to drink a lot sometimes," "used to bring some real floozies home sometimes," "used to fish at night," "must've had fifteen heads . . . animals I didn't even know the names of"—what did all that add up to?

And how had Janeski described him? Hell, Balzic

thought, Janeski hadn't described him—he'd just reacted to his name. The closest Janeski had come to describing him was with that name he'd almost called him.

And why had Peluzzi's face lost its color at the mere mention of Gallic's name?

And why did two men who spent as much time with a third as those two had with Gallic suddenly stop seeing him?

". . . he must've had fifteen heads," Mickey Samarra had said, meaning, of course, the animals Frank Gallic had killed, but Balzic couldn't help wondering how many heads Frank Gallic had. How many and which ones did he show to Mickey Samarra? How many and which to Janeski and Peluzzi? How many and which to Tina Samarra?

So we come back to that, Balzic thought. No matter how many other questions rocketed around in his mind, that one always returned to push aside the others: how many heads did Gallic show Tina? How many, that she should insist that all those other heads, those mounted ones, had to be thrown out? How many, that Gallic's pickup truck should appear to her—according to her brother—not to exist? How many, that, after a month after Gallic had not appeared after that fishing trip to Tionesta, she should go to Toledo and stay for a year? How many, that she should come back, again according to her brother, without announcing her intention to come back? How many, that she should move into the place where Gallic had lived, into the trailer where the two of them had spent how much time together and how many nights?

Balzic slammed the trunk lid and got behind the wheel of his car.

Mickey, he thought, she's your sister, and I respected your wish not to bother her before, but, dammit, I have to talk to her. Maybe she won't let me in that trailer, but in the yard, in the business, in this car, somewhere, she's going to talk to me. Somewhere, somehow, whether she wants to or not, she's going to tell me why she's living in that trailer.

It was ten minutes after twelve when Balzic pulled into

Galsam's parking lot. He had just put his hand on the door handle to get out when his call signal came over the radio.

"Balzic here," he said into the mike.

"Lieutenant Minyon here, Balzic. We got lucky today. I thought you might be interested."

"How so?"

"The dogs turned up another bone a little after eight this morning, and I had one of my people run it over to the coroner."

"Same fit?"

"The same, but not the same. This one, the tibia, Grimes calls it, the left calf bone—turns out it was broken once, fairly recently. Within the past four or five years. That was Grimes's first guess."

"And?"

"Grimes X-rayed it and that confirmed the break. Then he checked with all the orthopedic surgeons in the area—turns out there are only six who specialize. Well, he just called me." Minyon paused.

Balzic could picture the expression of satisfaction behind that pause. "So what did he come up with?"

"Our bones finally have a name," Minyon said. "And strangely enough, that name is on the list you left with Bielski for me."

Balzic could not put up with Minyon's dramatic pauses any longer. "It was Gallic, right?"

The pause this time, if such could be said, was filled with disappointment. "How the hell did you know?"

"He was the only one it could've been," Balzic said. "Everybody else was accounted for."

"And just what else do you know that you haven't told me? What have you been doing?"

"Not much. Just sort of driving around. Why?"

"Well do you think you might be able to drive in here and tell me what this information you asked Bielski to get for you—what it has to do with everything? I'd like to know."

"So would I. I mean, I don't know what it means. I'll be in in a little while. I have to do some shopping now."

"Some what?"

"Shopping. You know, buying food for the table. I don't know about you, but I eat every once in a while. See you when I get there. Out." Balzic replaced the mike on its hook and got out while Minyon was still demanding him to come in.

Up yours, Jack, Balzic thought, and got out of the car. He went into the service section of Galsam's—where he'd talked to Mickey Samarra earlier—just as Tina Samarra was leaving her trailer.

He watched her come across the gravel drive. Stramsky had described her well: her face, though feminine and more comely, had as many hard edges as her brother's; she was short and sturdily built; she wore a white dress of the kind worn by waitresses and beauticians; and the white, low-heeled shoes and flesh-colored stockings she wore accentuated her very muscular calves. There was not a suggestion of make-up on her face, and her hair was cut short enough so that she probably never did anything but run a comb through it in the mornings. Pulled around her shoulders was a heavy wool sweater which she clutched at her throat. She passed the pickup truck—as Mickey had earlier tried to explain to Balzic—as though it wasn't there.

She paid no attention to Balzic until she'd gone through the levered door in the counter and put her sweater on a shelf under the counter. "Yes, sir," she said, "can I help you?" There wasn't a trace of a smile of salesmanship.

Balzic produced his ID. "I'd like to ask you some questions," he said after allowing her time to study the picture on his ID and compare it to his face.

Just then Mickey Samarra, his apron and sleeves smeared with blood, came through the wooden door in the back wall behind his sister. "Oh, you're here, Tina. I didn't—Mario, I didn't know it was you," he said.

"How would you?" Tina said. "You just got here. You got

a peephole in the wall?" She had not turned around. Her gaze, curious about Balzic yet somehow remote, had not left Balzic's face.

Mickey shrugged as though to say to Balzic, you see? You see how she is? What did I tell you?

"I'd like to talk to Tina awhile, Mickey," Balzic said. "That okay with you?"

"If you want to talk to me, why don't you ask me?" Tina said. "Why are you asking him?"

"Because he's your—"

"My what? My brother?"

"Yes."

"That's right. That's what he is. No matter what he thinks he is, he's just my brother."

Mickey shook his head behind her, held up his arms, and let them drop to his sides. He turned, still shaking his head, and went out through the door he'd come in. Only then did Tina turn around, as though to be sure he'd gone. When she turned back, she folded her arms and waited, her eyes unwaveringly focused on Balzic's eyes.

"Mickey tells me, uh, you were supposed to get married."

"I was."

"You mind telling me what happened?"

"Yes, I mind. But that won't stop you. I can tell that. So the answer is you can't marry somebody who isn't there."

"Yes, but what I mean is, what happened? How come that somebody wasn't there?"

"That I wouldn't know."

"I'd ask him, you understand, but it seems he's not around."

"Looks like you're stuck then."

"You mean you have no idea why he's not around? You mean there was never any indication that he was going to not be around?"

"Oh, there were some indications all right. I just didn't pay attention to them. You never do, I hear. That's what it's supposed to be like, isn't it? Being in love? You don't see

what's there? At least that's what I was told." For the first
time, her face lost its stony composure. She smiled, but there
was no pleasure in it. It had the suggestion of something
more than irony, Balzic thought, but he hesitated to give it
a name, thinking he might be seeing more than was there.

"How long did you know him?"

"Since I was a kid. Seven, eight, I don't know. He was
always with Mickey. Since after the war."

"Mickey said you two didn't pay much attention to one
another until just a couple years ago. I think he said it was
three years ago."

"Mickey must've told you a lot."

"Well, not a lot, but some things."

"You talked to him long enough."

"Why? Were you watching us?"

"Watching other people is not my thing," she said. "I just
heard your car this morning. When you came, when you
left."

"Yeah, I guess it would be pretty hard not to hear. Your
trailer's pretty close."

"It's not my trailer."

"Yeah, I was going to ask you about that." Balzic watched
her face for some change, some twitch, some flicker of apprehension. She remained impassive.

"I've been living in it since I got back from Toledo.
Mickey would've told you that. He probably knows to the
hour how long. Probably has it written down on a little piece
of paper in his wallet."

"As a matter of fact, he has. Three months ago yesterday,
I think he said."

"Then he also told you I was living with our sister for a
year."

"Yeah, he told me that, too."

"I guess he told you just about everything."

"No, not everything."

"He wouldn't. He wouldn't tell you how many times I
slept with him."

"No, not how many times exactly. But he told me you did."

If that surprised her, she did not show it.

"Funny," Balzic said, "neither one of us has even said his name. For all we know, we could be talking about two different people."

"At least two different people," Tina said, "and there's nothing funny about it."

"No, I suppose there isn't. But just to keep things straight, I'm talking about Frank Gallic. That who you're talking about?"

"Yes."

"Just yes?"

"You asked me a question, I gave you an answer."

Balzic had to smile at that. He leaned on the counter and loosened his tie. "You know, there's a funny—well, not funny. Curious. There's a curious thing about this guy Gallic. I've talked to a couple of people about him, and all the people I talk to—except for Mickey, of course—they all don't seem to want to tell me one thing more than just exactly what I ask. You know what I mean? All except for Mickey."

"That's Mickey for you," Tina said, giving the faintest hint of a shrug.

"Mickey seems really baffled about the whole business. Hurt. And not just a little bit. Seems he's been hurt bad."

"No worse than anybody else. He just thinks so. Mickey just can't get over the idea he could do anything wrong."

"You knew better?" Balzic said quickly.

"I didn't say that. I—"

"I know what you said. What I asked you was whether you knew better."

"Any woman knows a man better than another man."

"Maybe so. But I'm not talking about any woman. Or any man. I'm talking about you and Frank Gallic."

"Then I'd still say the same thing."

"Which means, if I understand you, that you knew Gallic a lot better than Mickey did."

"Oh my God, anybody would know him better than Mickey did. Mickey's my brother, but he's dumb. All he knows is business. He's in his trailer, he's in here working, he goes to pick up the animals, he goes to the gas station, he goes to church. His whole life is right there."

"Yours isn't?"

"Now? I guess I'm no different, so I shouldn't talk."

"But it used to be different. When you were with Gallic?"

"You know the answer to that."

"Was it good?"

"What's that supposed to mean?"

"Just what it sounds like. Was your life good with him?"

"For a while, yes, I suppose."

"What changed it?"

"I don't know. I saw some things."

"Like what things?"

"Things things. I don't remember. I just saw some things."

"For somebody who claims a woman knows a man better than any man, you aren't too specific."

"I don't like to talk about it. When you don't like to talk about something, it gets sort of fuzzy. You forget the things you don't want to talk about, and pretty soon you don't even remember what you were trying to forget—if you're lucky."

"Well, if you don't mind, I'd like you to try and remember those things."

"Sure you would. That's what all you . . ."

"All you what? All you men? That what you were going to say?"

"What if I was?"

"Well, just because one man goes bad on you, especially when you thought he was good, that doesn't mean all men are bad, does it?"

"I'd like to hear what the women you know would say about that."

"I've got a mother, a wife, and two daughters. They all live with me, and I don't think they think I'm too bad. I could be kidding myself," Balzic said, smiling.

"You probably are."

"Oh, you got it bad. He must've been a real bastard. Underneath, I mean."

"You wouldn't have had to go too deep."

"But there was something about him. There must've been something good about him, otherwise, you wouldn't be as mad as you are."

"Mad isn't the word for it."

"What is the word then?"

Tina's gaze for the first time left Balzic's eyes. She looked out the large plate-glass window in the direction of the trailer. Then she turned back to Balzic, but she said nothing, looking at him again as she had all along, directly in the eyes.

"What's the word, Tina?"

She said nothing.

"Okay," Balzic said, "so when was the last time you saw him?"

"Over a year ago. Fifteen, sixteen months, I don't know. Mickey would know. He has it written down in his wallet."

"He left to go fishing on the twenty-sixth of July. It was a Friday. The following Monday morning, the truck was here, but he wasn't. That's what Mickey told me. Now when was the last time you saw him?"

Before she could answer, a state police cruiser wheeled into the parking lot. The doors flew open and stayed open. Two troopers got out of the front seat and Lieutenant Minyon got out of the back. He led the troopers in.

"Lieutenant," Balzic said, nodding to Minyon.

Minyon ignored Balzic and spoke to Tina. "I'm looking for a Michael Samarra. Would you please get him."

Balzic looked at the paper folded in Minyon's hand. He knew what it was, but he didn't want to believe it. "What do you have there, Lieutenant?"

"I asked you to please notify Michael Samarra that I want to see him," Minyon said to Tina. To the two troopers he said, "Check around back and in the trailers."

"Just a minute," Tina said, "I'll get him." She reached under the counter for a small intercom phone and said into it, "Mickey, come out front."

"What do you got there?" Balzic repeated to Minyon.

"That should be obvious," Minyon said. "Later on, chief, you can explain to me why you didn't come back to the barracks when I asked you. For now, I'll tell you that I didn't appreciate your little joke about shopping. I'll also tell you there are a couple of things you better tell yourself."

"Oh yeah? Like what things?"

"Like who you are and who I am."

"Oh? I, uh, thought I had a pretty good idea who—"

He didn't get to finish. Mickey Samarra came in then, wiping his hands on his apron, looking quite stupefied at the sight of the three state policemen.

"What—what's the matter?"

"Are you Michael Samarra?" Minyon said.

Mickey swallowed and nodded. "Yes—yes. I am."

"I have a warrant for your arrest. It is my duty to inform you that you are entitled to remain silent, that you are entitled to legal counsel, and that anything you say may be used against you in a court of law. Do you understand the rights I've just explained to you?"

"Mario," Mickey said, "what's he talking about?"

"Do you understand your rights as I have explained them to you?" Minyon said, emphasizing each syllable.

"Just tell him you understand, Mickey," Balzic said.

"Okay. I—sure," Mickey said. "I understand. But how come? What for?"

"You're under arrest for suspicion of the murder of one Frank Joseph Gallic."

"The what?" Mickey said, blanching.

Balzic kept watching Tina. She didn't move, she hardly blinked while the two troopers, at Minyon's direction, led Mickey out to their cruiser.

Minyon said at the door, "You've still got some explaining to do, Balzic."

"Don't I know it," Balzic said.

"Men," Tina said, picking up her sweater and thrusting her arms into the sleeves. "Well," she said to Balzic, "what are you waiting for?"

"I was waiting to see what you were going to do."

"Jesus Christ," she said, "what do you think I'm going to do? I'm going with him." Before she could arrange the closed sign in the window of the front door, the state police cruiser was backing out of the lot. She jerked open the door and shouted, "Wait!" but Minyon ignored her and ordered the trooper driving to get going.

"Come on," Balzic said, "I'll drive you."

"You bastards probably had it planned this way," Tina said.

"You can think what you want," Balzic said, going out to his car, "but I give you my word, I didn't have anything to do with this. I'm as surprised as you are."

"I'll just bet you are." She made sure the door was locked and then hurried over to the trailer. In a few seconds she was out, carrying a small black purse. She stopped to make doubly sure the trailer door was locked, pulling on it and twisting the knob each time. She had barely closed the car door when she said, "Well? What the hell are you waiting for? They'll have him talking in circles in five minutes."

Balzic knew better than to try to pick up where they'd been when Minyon came marching in on them. At first he wanted to try, but when he could hear the noises she made smoking, he knew it would be less than useless. He could only aggravate her into a deeper resistance, and that was the one thing he did not want to do.

In the parking lot at the state police station she turned to him and said, "If you know a lawyer—a good one—I'd appreciate it if you'd get him."

It surprised him. He had assumed she didn't allow herself the luxury of asking favors. "For Mickey?" he said.

"For who else?" she said, slamming the door and breaking into a run across the lot and up the steps into the station.

Balzic got Sergeant Angelo Clemente on the radio and told him to locate Mo Valcanas. "God knows where he'll be," Balzic said. "If he isn't in court or in his office, try Muscotti's or the back room of the bowling alleys. Rocksburg Bowl. When you get him, tell him an innocent citizen is being persecuted by the state police. That should get his ass in gear."

Balzic could have tried himself to locate Valcanas from inside the station, but he didn't want to miss more than he had to. It was going to be interesting to see how Minyon handled this. For a very brief moment, Balzic almost felt a twinge of sympathy for Minyon. The pompous ass had no idea what he had let himself in for with Tina Samarra. Ah well, Balzic thought as he went inside to the duty room, it'll serve him right.

Corporal Ed Bielski was standing at the front counter rubbing his eyes when Balzic walked in.

"S'matter, Ed," Balzic said in a low voice, "got something in your eye?"

"Yeah," Bielski said. "A lieutenant."

"Where are they?"

"In his office, I guess."

"Ed, a couple of things. What kind of warrant did he have?"

"John Doe."

"So he hasn't notified the DA's office yet?"

"Hell, no."

"One more thing. How did he manage to jump to the conclusion that his man was Samarra? Was it from what the savings and loan said?"

"How he jumps anywhere is something you have to ask him. But if you mean did he get the idea from that, I'd have to say yes. He stood around for a couple of minutes after he called you, then he snapped his fingers, and he was off."

"Thanks, Ed," Balzic said, ducking under the counter. He leaned close to Bielski in passing and said, "Just keep in mind there's always the chance he could get killed in the line of duty."

"His kind never gets killed for crissake," Bielski said. "What I'm hoping for is somebody'll offer me a job as head guard at a hospital or something."

Balzic made his way around the desk and down the short corridor to Minyon's office. He opened the door quietly and stepped inside and took an unobtrusive position in a corner next to a filing cabinet.

Tina Samarra, arms folded and clutching her purse, her face as impassive as ever, had stationed herself at her brother's side. Minyon sat on the front edge of his desk and worked a pencil in his hands as though it were a swagger stick. Mickey Samarra, still in his work clothes, the smell of blood and cow dung fresh on him, sat stiffly on a straight-backed chair, his thick hands on his knees.

". . . and you're trying to tell me that your partner has been missing for more than fifteen months and you never once thought to call the police?" Minyon said.

"You don't have to answer that," Tina said, as the stenographer worked to keep up.

"Tina, please," Mickey said, his eyes rolling.

It struck Balzic that Mickey may have been around cattle too long; his eyes had taken on the bovine cast of dull apprehension.

"This is the last time I'm going to warn you, miss," Minyon said, holding his gaze on Mickey as he spoke, "you interrupt again and I'm going to have you put out of this room, bodily if necessary."

"Sure, that's right. Threaten me," Tina said. "But I heard what you said about his rights, and you can't promise him those things one minute and take them away the next."

"Tina, please," Mickey said. "I know what he said. I got nothing to hide."

Minyon pressed a button on his intercom. "I want two men in here," he said.

"Sure!" Tina snapped. "Get two more. That's just perfect. Why don't you bring all your friends in? Give everybody a chance!" Her face twisted in fury.

Again Balzic was surprised. He had not thought her likely to lose control. Yet the more closely he watched her in the next few seconds, the less certain he was that she *had* lost control. If anything, her fury seemed fully under control, and the more furious for it.

The door opened and two troopers, both over six feet tall, came in.

"You better not let them touch me," Tina said to Minyon, "or so help me God, you'll be sorry."

"Get her out of here," Minyon said, turning his back on them and walking around his desk to look out a window.

The first trooper reached out to put his hand on Tina's arm. She whipped her purse across his face. Before he could back away, she kicked him in the shin and started him hopping. The second trooper had started to move toward her, but apparently thought better of it.

Balzic glared at Minyon's back, swore to himself, and stepped between the two troopers and Tina. Mickey by this time was up and confronting the troopers, the cow-like glaze in his eyes turned to something bullish.

"Hold it!" Balzic said. "Everybody just hold it. Sit down, Mickey. Everything's all right." Balzic bent down to pick up Tina's purse and handed it to her.

"I said to remove her," Minyon said, his back still to them. "And remove Balzic too."

"Uh, lieutenant," the second trooper said, "which one is that?"

Minyon spun around. "Who's in charge here?" he shouted. "I am! Get that woman and that man out of here!" His right arm shot out, the pencil quivering at Balzic.

"That's right. I'm Balzic and he's in charge. Tina, come along. We don't want to make things more difficult than they are. Come along, it's all right. Mickey doesn't have anything to hide. He'll be all right."

"Out!" Minyon roared. "And you. Samarra! Sit down!"

"Come on, Tina," Balzic said, holding out his hand to guide her out the door but being careful not to touch her.

"Mickey," Tina said as she started for the door, "you remember what he said before, this big man. This real big man. You don't have to say anything."

"Tina, I don't have nothing to hide," Mickey said, his eyes going soft again.

"After you," Balzic said to the two troopers, the one having a time trying to walk and rub his shin.

"And book her for assaulting a police officer," Minyon said as the four of them left the office.

"Don't bother," Balzic said after he'd closed the door.

"What do you mean, don't bother?" the first trooper said. "She could've put my eye out with that damn purse."

"'Cause I'm a witness," Balzic said, "that's why don't bother. You'll tell one story, your partner'll tell one, she'll tell one, and I'll tell another. And believe me, I know the magistrates in this town better than you two do. Better than Minyon does. Believe me, it won't get past the magistrate's office, so what's the point?"

"He's the point," the second trooper said, pointing with his thumb toward Minyon's closed door.

"Ah, forget him. You two hang around here long enough, you'll be looking for something to book him on, so let's just forget it, all right? Let me worry about him. Go talk to Corporal Bielski. He'll tell you about me. In case you don't know, I'm chief of police here."

The troopers looked at one another. The trooper Tina kicked said, "I hope you know what you're doing. As for you, sister, you better thank somebody I got a lot of patience."

"I'm not your sister, and from the looks of you, I'd say patience was all you had."

Balzic winced. "Okay, Tina, that's enough. It's over now. Let's just forget it, okay? What do you say?"

"Tell them," she said.

"Go on, fellas. Go talk to Bielski. He'll tell you I know what I'm doing. And if you don't believe him, go talk to Ralph Stallcup."

"I don't know," the first trooper said, rubbing his face where he'd been hit by the purse and glaring at Tina.

"I say we go talk to Bielski," the other trooper said.

"Okay. But I'm telling you, lady—"

"You can't tell me anything, buster. You ever put your hands on me again, you'll get a lot worse."

"For your information, dearie, I didn't touch you."

"Like hell you didn't. You grabbed me. Right here," Tina said, holding up her left arm.

"Enough, for crying out loud," Balzic said. "Tina, here. Sit down over here. Go on, you two. Go talk to Bielski."

The troopers shrugged at one another and walked off toward the duty room, the one still favoring his leg and rubbing his face.

Balzic pointed to one of the three chairs along the wall outside Minyon's office. "Have a seat, Tina. Go on."

"I'll stand."

"Okay, suit yourself. I got to tell you something, though. That trooper was right. He never touched you."

"He was going to. That's the same thing."

"Uh, maybe you think so, but I'll tell you what. If it ever really came down to it in a magistrate's office, I couldn't lie about it."

"Then why'd you tell them you would? You looking for something?"

"Oh for crissake," Balzic said, sitting in the chair closest to Minyon's door and putting his face in his hands. "You don't quit, do you?"

"I will," she said, looking straight ahead. "When I'm ready."

"What does that mean?"

"I'll tell you that, too. When I'm ready."

Balzic tried again to study her face, and again had to give it up without coming to any satisfactory conclusion. An idea was beginning to form though, murky and with only a few clear edges, and he was trying to help it along without knowing what it was when Minyon's voice carried through the door.

"You're lying!" Minyon shouted.

Balzic turned in the chair and put his ear close to the door.

"I swear to you on my mother's grave I wouldn't do that to Frank," came Mickey's voice. "Frank was my friend. We went through a war together . . . we were partners for twenty-five years—"

"And you were tired of having a partner!"

"Why? Why would I get tired of that? I didn't want nothing. I had everything I want. My God, you said you checked our savings. You had to see I had more than Frank. . . ."

"That son of a bitch," Tina said.

Balzic thought at first she'd meant Minyon, but when he looked up at her, he wasn't so sure. Had she meant Frank? He didn't know. All he knew for certain was that he had never met a woman before who was so able to conceal her thoughts. Had she worked at that? Or had circumstances forced the ability on her?

". . . had everything you want. Had! That's your word, Samarra," Minyon said. "I'm telling you, you didn't have everything you wanted. You wanted the business. All of it. All for yourself."

"But that's crazy. I paid taxes for Frank. I kept up his end. If I wanted the business, if I didn't want Frank for a partner no more, how come I did that? Mario told me I was nuts for doing that. And now you're telling me that's how you know I did . . ."

"Did what? What did you do? Murder your partner? And then saw him up in little pieces? I know that much, Samarra. I know how your partner was taken apart. It was with a butcher's saw."

Balzic stood up. "Listen, Tina, I'm going out front and make a phone call. Do yourself a favor. You and Mickey. Don't go back in there, will you?"

She said nothing for a moment. Then, as though she had not heard him, she asked, "Did you get a lawyer?"

"I didn't call him, no, but I told somebody to call him. He's a tough man to find sometimes. But he'll be here, don't worry about that. Okay? Just don't go back in there."

"Go make your phone call and leave me alone."

"All right," Balzic said. "All right. I'll leave you alone." He went out to the duty room, saw the two troopers huddled with Bielski in a far corner, and went to the opposite side of the room and dialed the coroner's office. A secretary answered.

"This is Mario Balzic. I'd like to ask Dr. Grimes some questions."

There was a click, a pause, and then Grimes said, "Mario, what can I do for you?"

"Answer a couple questions. Number one, how are you so positive the bones used to be Frank Gallic? I mean, I don't doubt it for a second, but I just want to know how positive you are."

"His tibia was fractured, Mario. I called all the orthopedic people I knew and had them check their records. Joe Statti was the one who came up with it. He remembered setting a tibia on about that approximate place four years ago. He brought his X rays over, and it was a simple matter. We just put one picture on top of the other and they matched."

"No possibility that somebody else could have had a break just like it?"

"Like it, yes. But not exactly like it. I imagine a professional oddsmaker would give you a million to one that two fractures would occur in the same way on the same place on the same bone, but he'd be leading a sucker on. The odds are more like a couple hundred million to one. There's no question about it. Even a layman would recognize it. All he'd have to do is look at the pictures."

"Okay. The second thing is, have you figured out what kind of instrument was used to saw them? Could you be sure of that?"

"No. All I can say with certainty is that it was some kind of fine-toothed saw."

"You wouldn't say it was a butcher's saw?"

"Mario, if you sent that question to the FBI, and you gave them enough time and enough different saw blades and enough bones to make a statistically satisfactory comparison, maybe you could get one of their people to testify to that effect. But I'm not going to get on any witness stand in any court and make any such statement. Even if I wanted to find out, I just don't have the equipment here or the time to make such an investigation."

"Then where the hell is Minyon getting the idea that it was a butcher's saw?"

"I suggest you ask him," Grimes said. "All I can tell you is that he didn't get it from me."

"Okay, Doc. Thanks. Sorry to bother you."

"No bother. Sorry I can't tell you what you want to know."

Balzic hung up and started past Bielski and the two troopers.

"What's General Minyon doing now?" Bielski said.

"The general. Yeah," Balzic said. "I guess that's what he's trying to do—make general. But I'll tell you what. All he's doing is making an ass out of himself. Which won't take too much doing."

Balzic was about to start down the corridor when he was hailed from behind. Myron Valcanas, listing a couple degrees to the right, his black fedora askew, eyes flecked red, a bandage across the brow of his right eye, put his hands on the counter and let out a long, ginny breath.

"Mario, just where the hell is this citizen who's being persecuted by these boy scouts?"

"Oh shit," Bielski said.

"Who's that?" the trooper who'd been kicked asked.

"That, young buddy, is the champion drunk of Conemaugh County, and he just loves us," Bielski said.

"He a lawyer?"

"Yeppie. And oh would I like to be there when he gets hold of Minyon."

"Back here, Mo," Balzic said.

Valcanas came through the counter door in the shuffling gait of one whose nerve ends had long since been burned ragged by alcohol. He tipped his hat to a typist. "Madam," he said, "how nice to see a flower among so many weeds."

The typist, a plain, plump woman, blushed and chewed her lower lip.

"Gentlemen," Valcanas said to Bielski and the other troopers, "how reassuring to know there are still weeds."

"Afternoon, Mo," Bielski said.

"Is that you, Bielski? Christ, you're so drunk I can hardly see you."

"What happened to your eye?"

"What else? A woman happened to it," Valcanas said, grinning. "What else ever happens to a man's eye? In the South, they call it reckless eyeballing, and you can get thirty days for it. Ten years if you're a nigger. Since I'm only a Greek, all I got was some knuckles. Only in saloons is justice so swift."

"Down here, Mo," Balzic said, trying to steer him.

"I heard you before for crissake. I'm coming."

Balzic led the way down the short corridor to where Tina Samarra was standing.

"This is the lawyer you sent for?" she said.

"Occasionally, madam, I am a lawyer. And what can I do for you, whoever you are?"

"This is Miss Tina Samarra, Mo. Her brother's inside with Lieutenant Minyon."

"I asked you to get a good lawyer," Tina said. "The least you could've done was get a sober one."

"Madam," Valcanas said, "let's get a few things straight. Number one, nobody says you have to hire me, and number two, nobody says I have to work for you. Since I seem to recall something a moment ago about somebody's brother being somewhere with some lieutenant, I'm presuming that you don't need to make any decision about hiring me, nor do I have to decide whether to work for you. In other words, keep your opinions regarding my sobriety to yourself. I've taken enough crap from women today—from them, about them, and because of them."

"Mo, a minute," Balzic said.

"Men," Tina said, turning away.

"Take two minutes, Mario. Just try to be concise is all I ask."

"Okay. Her brother Mickey is under arrest for suspicion of the murder of his business parter, one Frank Gallic. . . ." Balzic went on to summarize the case to this point. He did not elaborate on the presence of Peluzzi and Janeski, nor did he offer a theory of his own about the murder. He ended by saying, "All I'll say for certain is Gallic has been dead for fifteen months, give or take a couple weeks, and her brother didn't do it."

"Just how are you so sure he didn't?"

"I know him, that's all."

"That's going to impress the hell out of a jury, Mario."

"That wasn't meant to impress any jury. That was just meant for you."

"Nonetheless, I hope to Christ you have more to base your opinion on than just your feeling about her brother."

"I do."

Valcanas started to say something else but stopped when Minyon's voice came resounding through the door: "You're lying! When are you going to stop lying?"

"The lieutenant?" Valcanas said, nodding toward the door.

"That's him."

"Madam," Valcanas said, "until such time as a decision is made to the contrary, I am your brother's lawyer." He stepped to the door and was about to knock. He turned to Balzic and said, "Christ, that sounded almost biblical, you know? If my mother could hear me now." He pounded on the door with his palm.

There were some impatient, heavy steps, and then the door was jerked open. Minyon stood there, flushed and sweating, looking Valcanas up and down.

Valcanas spoke very softly. "Sergeant, my name is Myron Valcanas and I'm an attorney. I believe you have just called my client a liar, and I'd like to speak with him. What I want to speak with him about is this: you have apparently been calling him names for some time without benefit of counsel, and I'd at least like to be able to explain to him the meaning of those names. Just a minor technicality, you understand."

"In the first place, it's lieutenant," Minyon said. "In the second—"

"Lieutenant? How dumb could I be?" Valcanas said. "Here I was, looking at your face, when all I had to do was look at your uniform. Now what was the second thing you wanted to say?"

"Are you drunk?"

"I'm hardly ever anything else. Is that the second thing?"

Minyon's mouth started to work as though he were chewing a sentence and didn't know whether to swallow it or spit it out. He stood a full five seconds like that and then stepped back slowly out of the doorway, allowing Valcanas to enter, shutting the door quickly behind him.

For fifteen minutes, Valcanas's voice could be heard, never loud enough for his words to be understandable, but without interruption. Then there was a pause, the door was jerked open again, and Valcanas led Mickey Samarra out of the office.

Balzic got a glimpse of Minyon before he slammed the

door. Minyon, poor Minyon, Balzic thought. He looked as though he needed to see a doctor about his blood pressure; his face was an unhealthy splash of blotches.

In the parking lot Balzic asked, "How the hell'd you get him out of there? He didn't have to let him go."

"That's right, he didn't," Valcanas said. "All I did was explain to him that anything my client had said under those circumstances wouldn't count for anything anyway. I mean, it wouldn't have mattered if he had made a full confession —assuming he had done it. As long as he didn't have legal counsel when he made it, it wouldn't be worth the paper it was written on."

"But hell, he knew that much."

"Certainly he did," Valcanas said. "But I have yet to see one of these boy scouts behave as though they really understood those rights they have to proclaim every time they make an arrest. They say all the words, but then they go right on as they always have, like they're in a goddamn Jimmy Cagney movie from out of the thirties. They make my ass tired. But the son of a bitch didn't understand me anyway."

"So what did you say that made him understand?"

"All I asked him finally was why he hadn't bothered to have the man arraigned. I mean, if he was all that goddamn sure the man was lying and had, in fact, done this terrible thing, then, hell, why not file the information against him? Of course, he had no answer. Thus, here we are in the parking lot. Now, who the hell's going to buy the next round?"

Mickey and Tina were standing beside them taking it all in, and Mickey, his face purest bovine befuddlement, said, "I told him I didn't do it. What was he hollering at me like that for? Jeez, I never been called a liar so many times in my life. My God, how does he think it feels—one minute I find out my partner's dead. The next minute he's screaming at me I killed him. My God, I loved Frank." With the last, he started to cry.

"Stop it," Tina snapped. "Jesus Christ, stop it!"

"Tina, don't talk to me like that. He was like my brother," Mickey sobbed.

"I know what he was like," Tina said, taking Mickey's arm and shaking him as though he were a child. She looked at Balzic. "Well. How do we get home? Do we have to walk?"

During the drive out to Galsam's Freezer Meats, Mo Valcanas asked to be filled in on the rest of the details. "As long as there's a possibility I might have to defend you, I ought to know what I'm going to defend you against," he said.

Mickey, sitting in the front seat with Balzic, did most of the talking, digging into his wallet to find the corroborating dates to his account of what had happened to Frank Gallic. Balzic glanced now and then into the rear-view mirror and saw Valcanas taking it all in. Once when Balzic glanced at the mirror, he could see Valcanas, still listening to Mickey, giving a long look at Tina. Balzic could not pick her up in the mirror. Apparently she had pressed herself against the opposite door, and because she said nothing during the entire drive, Balzic found himself wondering momentarily whether she was still with them. A foolish thought, he knew.

". . . was I wrong about the taxes?" Mickey was asking Valcanas as Balzic pulled onto the gravel of Galsam's parking lot.

"Not at all," Valcanas replied. "You were just trying to keep the business going. It's not exactly the way I would've done it, but if anything, it speaks in your favor. What doesn't, though, is the fact that you didn't call the police. Course you said you attempted to find him through Missing Persons. There again, that isn't, as some assistant DA would say, the act of a prudent, reasonable man who has nothing to hide. But at least you made that much of an effort."

They got out after a moment when nobody said anything.

Tina, after nodding to Balzic in what he supposed was an expression of gratitude for getting her brother out of the hands of the state police, turned without a word and went immediately into her trailer. After she was gone Balzic wondered whether her nod had been intended to mean gratitude or simply good-bye.

Mickey hooked his stubby thumbs in the pockets of his butcher's coat and shuffled about. "What do I do now? Just go back to work? How can I do that? My God . . ."

"I don't think you have anything to worry about," Balzic said, knowing as the words left his lips how asinine they must have sounded.

"Nothing to worry about!" Mickey cried out. "How can you say that? My partner is dead. Murdered! A crazy man, a state police—he accuses me! My God . . ."

"I didn't mean that the way it came out," Balzic said. "What I meant was I know you didn't have anything to do with it."

Mickey stopped shuffling. "How do you know? Tell me, my God. I want to hear. I have to hear!"

"I just know, that's all," Balzic said, taking Mickey's hand and shaking it. "Take my word for it." He nodded to Valcanas and they got back in the car.

As they drove off, Mickey seemed to Balzic to be standing like a bagged tree in a nursery, its roots close to the ground but surrounded by burlap; Mickey knew where he was supposed to be but seemed to have no comprehension of how to do what he knew he ought to be doing.

"What do you make of it, Mo?"

Valcanas shook his head. "The only thing I can say right now is that I tend to agree with you about him. He seems as unlikely a murderer as I've ever seen. But there are so damn many things that don't make sense."

Balzic snorted his agreement with that.

"For instance, he—Mickey—claims something happened

on that fishing trip, but the first question that comes to my mind is how his truck got back here."

"Well, that notion of his about something happening on that trip doesn't hold for a couple reasons. I'm not saying nothing happened, understand, but it's pretty hard for me to believe that somebody would kill this guy a hundred miles away and then cart the body all the way back here to get rid of it."

"Just where did they get rid of it? Or he, or she, or whoever."

"I forgot. You don't know that."

"Hell, I don't know anything. Where was it found?"

"In the first place, it hasn't all been found. And all that has been found was scattered all over seven or eight farms that were leased by the Police Rod and Gun Club."

"You mean it was dismembered."

Balzic nodded.

"Well, then, that explains why that idiot lieutenant jumped on Samarra. You have a dismembered corpse, go find somebody used to dismembering corpses, especially if that somebody is the corpse's business partner."

"Yeah, but the thing about that is, as far as I know, Mickey's never been on those farms. He's not a member of the club. Never was. Hell, I doubt that he ever hunted. Gallic was the hunter."

"How about the other two—the ones he went on that fishing trip with?"

"Janeski and Peluzzi."

"Yeah. Those two. So the guy was fishing with them and that's presumably the last anybody saw of him. Were they members of the club?"

"They were. But they both quit. Said Gallic talked them into a commercial preserve up around Indiana someplace."

"I take it you've talked to them."

"Oh, sure. But it was like pulling teeth. I'll skip the details, but they both gave me the impression that something happened that weekend they don't want to talk about. And they also didn't want to talk about Gallic any more either."

"You don't sound as though you tried too hard, Mario."

"I didn't really. Course when I was talking to them, I didn't know Gallic was our corpse either. So I didn't really know what I was talking to them about."

"Well, I don't want to tell you how to run your business, but it seems pretty goddamn obvious you're going to have to turn the heat on them."

"Oh, don't worry about that. I intend to," Balzic said. "But, uh, the thing I'd like to know is what you think of her. Tina."

"Offhand, I'd say she was one of those puritanical Italian females, the kind that look like they ought to be great in the hay until some poor sap gets in there and finds out he's trying to make love with somebody that should've been a nun. I know a lot of Greek females like that, and to my mind, there's no worse breed than a Mediterranean body parading around under a Victorian head."

"I guess I could learn something from that if I knew what the hell it meant. Mediterranean bodies I understand. Victorian heads I don't."

"Neither does anybody else," Valcanas said. "You understand puritan, don't you?"

"Yeah."

"Well, the best definition of a Victorian I ever heard was a person who looked at his genitals and never really believed they belonged to him—as opposed to a puritan who knew they were his and wished to hell they weren't. Oh hell, I'm starting to sound like some goddamn professor for crissake."

"In other words, you think she's not really happy about being a woman?"

"What do I know? Hell, I've seen her only those few minutes. One thing I'm sure of. The only way she could've been any farther away from me on the way out to their place was to get out and ride on the fender."

"Well, then what do you think of this? She made her brother get rid of all Gallic's trophies—which he didn't do—yet she lives in Gallic's trailer."

"It's odd, no doubt about that. Did I hear somebody say they were supposed to get married?"

"Yeah, they were."

"Hell, it might be something as simple as her not having any other place to live. On the other hand, it might be as complicated as any psychiatrist could make it."

"She does have another place to live. Her brother's still got their parents' house up in Norwood. That's where she used to live. Then about a month after Gallic disappeared, she went to live with their oldest sister in Toledo. Then, three months ago, she came back and moved into Gallic's trailer."

"Who knows?" Valcanas said, stretching. "Who knows what women have in their heads. Freud didn't. And you can see from this patch over my eye that I'm not half as smart as he was. I'm just a small-town lawyer with a bottomless thirst. Speaking of that, how about dropping me at Muscotti's?"

Balzic turned north on Main and pulled over to the curb in front of Muscotti's Bar and Grille. "I meant to ask you before. How'd you get up to the state police?"

"Cab," Valcanas said, getting out. "You don't think I'm dumb enough to try driving in my condition, do you?" He started to shut the door and then leaned back in. "I'll tell you, Mario, if I were you, I'd really turn some pressure on those two Gallic went fishing with. And the other thing I'd do, I'd find out where Tina was living that month before she went to live with her sister. I don't know what there is about her, aside, that is, from what I've already said. But I'd sure as hell check her out. What am I talking about? This is your problem. I work the other corner."

"Exactly what kind of pressure would you put on those two—if you were me? I know what I'm going to do. I just want to see if you'd do something different."

"If I were you? Hell, everything I could think of. I'd make a real performance out of it. I'd pick them up on a John Doe, bring them in at the same time, and then separate them. Then? Then I'd shake my finger at them and tell them I know they're a couple of bad boys and need a good spanking." Valcanas grinned. "Can't talk you into a drink?"

"Nah, not now. Thanks anyway. You don't need my company."

"I don't need anybody's company. I get drunk enough, I don't even need my own. That's the whole idea." Valcanas straightened up and shut the door.

Balzic watched him shuffle into Muscotti's and then drove off to Magistrate Aldo Vallone's office to get a couple John Doe warrants.

Janeski was picked up just as he was punching the time clock to begin the second shift at the can factory. A beat patrolman who knew Peluzzi picked him up as he was coming out of the unemployment office after signing for his compensation check.

Balzic had Janeski kept in a car outside city hall until Peluzzi was brought in, and then had Janeski brought inside just as he was directing Peluzzi into an interrogation cubicle.

"What the fuck's going on?" Peluzzi said.

"Sit down, Peluzzi," Balzic said, shutting the door.

"You can't just grab us like this. What for?"

"Us? Who's us?"

"I didn't say us. Did I say us? I meant me."

"That's your first lie. Now sit down."

Peluzzi thought about it a moment, then took one of the two straight-backed chairs in the cubicle and straddled it. "You better watch out how you talk, Balzic, calling me a liar. I ain't no dummy. I read the papers. I know what kind of rights I got."

"Peluzzi, in the first place, those rights you're talking

about are for people who haven't done anything. But that doesn't include you, 'cause you're in a lot of trouble."

"I ain't in nothing."

"I know otherwise. Your pal's been talking."

"Don't give me that shit. What is this—the movies? Television? My pal's been talking. Shit. What pal?"

"The one that's been in here most of the afternoon. You know, the other one in the 'us' you were talking about a minute ago. Course you can go ahead and still try to make jokes if you want, but personally, I don't see a damn thing funny about Frank Gallic's murder."

Peluzzi had been searching through his pockets for a match. He froze at the word murder and stared incredulously at Balzic.

"What's the matter?" Balzic said. "Isn't it funny any more?"

"Hey, now wait a minute. Wait just a fucking minute."

"What for?"

"Say that again. Whose murder?"

"You heard me."

"I know I heard you. I just don't believe you."

"Okay, I'll say it again. It won't come out any different. Frank Gallic's murder."

"You got me in here for that? Man, I didn't even know he was dead." Peluzzi hadn't moved. Except for his mouth, he seemed locked in time, his hands trapped in his pockets, his unlit cigarette stuck to his lips.

Balzic lit the cigarette for him and pulled over an ash tray.

"You didn't know he was dead, huh? I suppose you didn't even know he hasn't been around for fifteen months, and I suppose you didn't know you and your pal Janeski were the last people to see him alive."

"Hey, come on, man, you're moving too fast."

"You come on. You and Janeski went fishing with Gallic up at Tionesta, a year ago this past July twenty-sixth. That was a Friday. On the following Sunday night Gallic's truck appears at his trailer beside his business, but that's all that shows up. Nobody's seen him since—nobody until a dog digs up one of his bones. That was on the first day of pheasant season. Now you tell me."

"Now, wait. Okay, so we went fishing. I'm not going to say we didn't. But that other thing, man, forget it. I didn't kill nobody. Never. Not even in the war. I was a radioman. I never shot at nothing in my life except animals."

"I didn't say anything about shooting anybody," Balzic said, letting it hang there.

"I didn't say you did. I'm just telling you I never did, that's all. What're you trying to do—get me all mixed up?"

"I don't have to try, Peluzzi. You're mixed up enough without any help from me. Now let's just see if you can get yourself unmixed enough to get your story straight."

"You mean you want to see if my story matches up with Janeski's."

"Did I say that? Now who's trying to get things mixed up?"

"Well what the fuck, man. You bring us both in here, you tell me he's been talking—about what I don't know—and then you hit me with this other noise. What am I supposed to think?"

"I don't care what you think, Peluzzi. Right now all I care about is what happened on that weekend you three were supposed to be fishing."

Peluzzi took a long drag on his cigarette and then tried to take it out of his mouth, but the paper stuck to his lips. The smoke curled into his nose and eyes, and his head jerked back.

Balzic, who had been standing, took the other chair and sat, removing his coat and loosening his tie before he did. "I'm waiting, Peluzzi."

Peluzzi picked at the paper on his lips and then went into a short spell of coughing. "Give me a second, man."

Balzic slapped the table and leaned forward. He said very loudly, "Give you a second! That's a laugh. Peluzzi, you're in trouble. We got some bones. Those bones used to be a man. That man used to be Frank Gallic. And you and your friend Janeski are the last two people to see Frank Gallic. We got a pathologist's report that says Frank Gallic, the guy you two went fishing with July twenty-six a year ago —a pathologist has it in writing that Frank Gallic's bones have been in the ground for fifteen months, and you sit there saying, 'Give me a second, man.'

"I'm tired of jokes, Peluzzi, and you damn well better get tired of them pretty quick, 'cause the way it stands right now, pal, you're up for this one."

"Balzic, honest to God, man, I didn't have nothing to do with that, I swear."

"You swear. Janeski swears. Both of you walking around with your hands on Bibles. Forget the swearing. I want to know what happened."

"What happened," Peluzzi said, his head going up and down and from side to side. "Nothing happened. We went fishing—"

"When? Exactly!"

"I don't know exactly. Late afternoon. Four, five o'clock. I don't remember."

"Janeski says it was three," Balzic lied.

"Okay, maybe it was three. I don't know. Christ, man, that was a long time ago. I can't even say for sure where I was three o'clock yesterday."

"Yesterday you got nothing to worry about. But from Friday to Sunday fifteen months ago you better start remembering. Okay, so you left. You say it was four or five. Janeski says three. So then what?"

"So we got there."

"When?"

"Nine, ten, I don't know. We stopped a couple places."

"Janeski says eight."

"Christ, I don't know," Peluzzi cried out. "I'm trying to tell you, man, that was a long time ago."

"So then what?"

"So then—so then we must've went fishing."

"Where?"

"I don't know, man. On the river. Somewhere. Christ, it was dark. Gallic was the one driving. I don't know where he parked."

"What—it stayed dark the whole time you were there? The sun didn't come up the next morning? Janeski says it was right in the middle of Nine Mile Run," Balzic said, making it up as he went along.

"Maybe it was. I'm not too good at places. Directions. If he says that's where we were, I guess it was. Tell you the truth, I was drinking beer all the way up. We could've been parked in New York for all I know."

"All right, so you don't know where. So you'd been drinking. So what do you remember?"

"I remember fishing and drinking, that's what I remember."

"The whole weekend? Just fishing and drinking? That's not what Janeski says."

"Yeah? Just what the fuck does he say?"

"You tell me. We both know something else went on besides fishing and drinking, Peluzzi. I know it. Janeski knows it. And you know it. You didn't spend the whole time up there just opening beer cans and tossing in a line. You did something else. What?"

"I don't remember."

"Janeski remembers. Why can't you?"

"Janeski, Janeski, Janeski! What's he remember? What?"

"That's what I want to hear from you."

Peluzzi said nothing. He took long drags on his cigarette, several in quick succession, and stared at the wall behind Balzic.

Balzic stood abruptly and put on his coat. "You think about it awhile, Peluzzi. I'll be back." He stepped out of the cubicle and shut the door behind him.

He went to the radio console where Vic Stramsky was sitting. "How much could he hear, Vic?"

"Probably a little less than I heard. And all I heard was you and him shouting a couple times. But I couldn't make out the words."

"You leave the door open?"

"Yeah. He tried to come out once. I told him to get his butt back in there and sit down."

"Good enough," Balzic said. "Do a favor, Vic. Two favors. One, call my wife and tell her I won't be home until pretty late. Two, if Minyon calls, I'm out chasing an accident."

Stramsky nodded and was reaching for a phone as Balzic walked into the cubicle where Richie Janeski was standing, head down, making a circle on the floor with the toe of his work shoe.

Balzic shut the door and took off his coat. "Have a seat, Janeski."

Janeski sat, folded his hands in his lap, and leaned back. His left knee started to bounce. He looked openly at Balzic but said nothing, his face locked into a sneer, making Balzic wonder how his life had been shaped by that.

Balzic reached around him on the chair and took his notebook out of his inside coat pocket. He pretended to read it for a minute and then put it back into his coat. He put his elbows on the table and said, "You married, Janeski?"

"Separated."

"Got kids?"

"Three."

"How old?"

"One girl's going to be fourteen, the boy's going on eleven, and the other girl's ten."

"How long you been separated?"

"Three years, give or take a couple weeks."

"That's a long time."

"It's three years, two weeks, and one day's worth of time, if you want to know."

"Oh," Balzic said. "It's like that?"

"Yeah, it's like that."

"Get to see your kids very much?"

"Yeah. Every week."

"I wonder what they're going to think when they find out about this."

"When they find out about what?"

"Frank Gallic's murder."

Janeski's knee stopped bouncing. His gaze, which had been fixed on Balzic's face, suddenly began to fly about the room. Otherwise, he remained motionless.

"You got nothing to say about it?" Balzic said.

"Hey, man. I told you before in Pravik's. I haven't seen that guy in over a year. I—"

"He's been dead over a year, Janeski. Fifteen months, more or less. The fact is, you're one of the last two people to see him alive. You and Axal Peluzzi."

"Well, what's that mean? Just 'cause we're the last to see him doesn't mean I killed him."

"I didn't say you did. Did I say that?"

"Never mind what you said. I can see what you're thinking. But I'll just tell you something you don't know. We weren't the last ones to see him. How about that?"

"I don't believe you."

"You can believe anything you want, man. I'm telling you we weren't the last."

"That's funny. That's not what Peluzzi says."

"I don't give a rat's ass what he said. How the hell would he know anything anyway? He was stoned."

"Then suppose you just tell me who this last person was to see Gallic."

Janeski started to chew his lips, his tongue flicking out and running over the scar that crossed his mouth. "I don't remember," he said after a long moment.

Balzic laughed. "Janeski, I'll tell you. I've seen some liars in here. All kinds. Real pros and real amateurs. But that one, that lie you just told, has got to rank right down on the bottom of the novice class. Maybe you don't understand some things, Janeski, and maybe you better start understanding.

"You and your friend Peluzzi, you're up for this. We have no other possibilities. Just you and him. You're it, pal. You're sitting there telling stupid lies, and you're about to stand up in front of a judge and hear that man say something terrible.

"Nobody's been in that chair down in Rockview for a couple years, Janeski, but I'll tell you, the way a lot of people are talking these days, hell man, certain people get themselves elected, they just might plug that chair in again. I'll tell you, I wouldn't want to be where you are, and I sure as hell wouldn't be sitting there telling dumb-ass lies."

Janeski's eyes had quit darting about and had fixed again on Balzic the while he was talking. For another long moment, Janeski said nothing, his tongue continuing to slide over his scar. Then he let out a long sigh and said, "There are worse things than dying, man."

Balzic waited nearly a minute before he spoke. "What's worse?" he asked softly.

"Lots of things, man," Janeski said barely above a whisper. "Lots of things . . . being lonely is worse. Being in a whole bunch of people and knowing they don't give two shits about you—that's worse. Not having a family is worse, man. And even worse than that is knowing you had a family and knowing you fucked it up, all by yourself, all because you acted stupid, that's worse. . . . I'll tell you straight, man, there've been plenty of nights I've been laying in bed and I'll be saying, 'Go ahead, get it over with. What the fuck, if this is what it's like, who needs it?' You don't know how many times I laid in bed and said that, man. . . ." Janeski's voice trailed off and his lips began to tremble.

"Why would you say that, Richie? What would make you want to say that? You do something wrong?"

"Aw, man. Wrong! Shit, I did a lot of things wrong. A ton. But one thing I didn't do, Balzic, and you can take it or leave it, man, 'cause I don't give a shit. I know what I did and I know what I didn't do. But one thing I didn't do, I didn't kill Frank Gallic. Maybe I should've, man. I'd be lying if I said I didn't want to. But I didn't, and those people you're talking about, they can plug that chair in and they can put me in it and when they turn it on, man, I'll be saying the same thing I'm saying now. I didn't kill him."

"You said maybe you should have. You said you'd be lying if you said you didn't want to," Balzic said, still speaking softly. It was not for effect. It had been earlier, but it wasn't now, because he could not recall seeing a man as young, as muscular, as seemingly full of health and strength as Janeski who was so clearly desperate. He could not imagine why he hadn't seen this about Janeski before in Pravik's, and the only reason he could give himself for not seeing it was the horrible and constant sneer on Janeski's face resulting from the scar and twisted nose.

"That's right," Janeski said. "That's what I said, and that's what I meant. 'Cause Gallic was no fucking good. It took me a long time to figure that out. Three years, two weeks, and one day, but I figured it out. I had plenty of time."

"How did you figure it out?"

"Oh man, are you kidding? I just told you. I see my kids once a week. Four hours I get to spend with them on Sundays. They're mine, man. I helped put them here. Four fucking hours a week. And my wife. My wife doesn't even look at me any more. Jesus . . ."

"I understand that, Richie, but, uh, what's that—"

"What's that have to do with wanting to kill Gallic?"

"Yes."

"Aw, shit, man, it's a long story. I don't even know all the parts. All I know is—well, fuck it, man—look at me. Look at my face. You know how long my face has been like this? You know how it got like this?"

Balzic waited.

"My old man did this to me. Yeah. My father. When I was six years old. I don't even remember what for. Maybe I didn't come fast enough when he called me or something. All I remember was one second I was on a scooter, man. Out on the sidewalk. One of those things with just a board

on some roller-skate wheels with a handle, and I was pushing myself along and he comes up behind me and raps me
across the back of the head and I go flying. The next thing
I know I'm all dizzy and throwing up from ether. I'm in a
hospital. And when they finally take the bandages off, man,
out I come. Like this. And all my life, man, I . . ." Janeski
buried his face in his hands and sobbed.

"Easy," Balzic said. "Easy now."

Janeski raised his head after a couple minutes and fumbled through his pockets for a hanky. He blew his nose and
wiped his eyes and then kept the hanky wadded up in his
right hand and worked it as though he was squeezing a rubber ball.

"You don't have to say any more about that," Balzic said.

"Why? 'Cause you think it doesn't have anything to do
with Gallic?"

"No, that's not why I said it. I said it because it's obviously very painful."

"Well it also has plenty to do with Gallic. And I know I
don't have to say anything more about it, man. I'm not
saying it because I have to. I'm saying it because I want to.
I never in my life told another man about this. The only
other person I ever told was my wife. I never even talked
about it with my mother, and my mother was there. My
mother, Jesus . . . You know what I told Gallic, not only
Gallic, but any guy that ever asked me about this? Boy, is
this a laugh. I used to tell guys I got this in a fight. I used
to tell them two niggers jumped me when I was in the Army.
And I used to tell them I kicked the shit out of those two
coons, man. Yeah. Feature that. I haven't been in a fight
in my life, since I was a kid, anyway. And what kind of
fights are kids' fights?

"But you know what really hurt," Janeski went on, "I
mean the worst of all? It was my mother, man. My mother
wouldn't even look at me, and every time she did, which
was an accident, she'd turn her face away, man, and I'd
run into the bathroom and look in the mirror and I used

to think, God, am I that ugly? And pretty soon I didn't even have to look in the mirror, man. I knew. I knew I was the ugliest kid in the whole motherfucking world.

"And the only thing good about it, man, was my old man finally left. Don't ask me why. I don't know. I been telling myself he left 'cause he couldn't stand to look at what he did to me, but I don't know if that's the truth. I'm probably just shitting myself. But he left anyway. I really didn't give a shit why. I was just glad he was gone. 'Cause I could never get near him, man. Never, without thinking he was going to maybe rap me and fuck me up all over again. And then there were times when he was still around, man, that I actually used to wish he would. Maybe the second time around he'd do it right. The whole job."

"Richie, you really don't—"

"If you're going to tell me again that I don't have to say this, I told you before, man I'm not doing what I don't want to do, okay? Just let me get this out once. I mean, just once, let me say the whole thing, okay?"

"Okay."

"So anyway, I met this girl. My wife. She was the first girl I ever met, man, that didn't look at me like I was Frankenstein. The only one, I swear. Skip the whores. All they look at is your money and your dick, see if you can pay and don't have anything.

"So I was out swimming at North Park. North Park was where I could go, you know? I started lifting weights early, man. That was something physical you could do all by yourself. You didn't have to put up with any shit from anybody in any locker room. All that rah-rah shit. I lifted weights for years, man, and when I'd go out North Park swimming, all those pretty boys, they didn't look so good beside me. I mean, swimming, man, when you're walking around in a bathing suit, if you're really built, maybe they don't notice your face so much—least that's what I used to tell myself.

"So anyway, I was out there swimming, and I was trying

to see how far I could make it across that pool under water. And I bumped into her. The funny thing was the water was up to my shoulders, so she couldn't see how I was built, and there she was still talking to me. It wasn't until we got out of the pool, man, that I see she only got one hand. All the time we were in the water, she couldn't see how I was built and I couldn't see she only got one hand, you get it?"

Balzic nodded.

"So everything goes along smooth, man. I mean, we understand one another. Why not? Who better than us? So we get married, I got a good job, the kids come along, I'm hunting and fishing when I want. I'm having a good time with my kids. We're living . . . and then about six years ago I met Gallic. I can't even remember how or where. Maybe Peluzzi introduced us. I can't even remember how I met Peluzzi. They're both a lot older than me, ten, maybe twelve years. Maybe it was in the club."

"The Rod and Gun Club?"

"Yeah. It had to be there. I just remember, it was either that time or another time, I was listening to Gallic talk. He just got back from Alaska. Shot a polar bear and he was talking about it. I don't know—he was a real talker. He could tell you anything and make you believe it. The thing was, most of the stuff he'd be telling you was true. But the thing I remembered most that first time I met him was he looked at me, square in the face, man, and he didn't say anything about my face. He didn't ask me about it until a long time later. And I remember thinking, listening to him talk, hey, he ain't such a bad guy. He spread the money around pretty good, and he listened when I said something. But most of all, he always looked at me when he was talking or listening.

"Next thing I know, we're buddying up—me, him, and Peluzzi.

"Then, pretty soon, I'm starting to spend more time with them, with Gallic, not with Peluzzi so much—I'm spending more time with him than I am with my own family. When I get a week's vacation, instead of taking my family somewhere, I'm going someplace with him. Canada four or five times. Alaska once. Christ, we even went to Mexico once. Supposed to hunt jaguars or mountain lions or something. What a joke that was. Cost me damn near a thousand bucks and all we got to show for it was . . ."

"Was what?" Balzic said.

"What? A dose of clap, that's what. From a couple whores in Juárez or someplace. I don't remember where. I just remember getting stoned on that tequila and ending up in this room with these two whores. Jesus, they were just kids. One of them couldn't have been thirteen. But there we were, me and Peluzzi and Gallic, taking turns. Taking turns with the whores and taking turns with the camera."

"With the what?"

"The camera. You know. A movie camera."

"Whose idea was that?"

"Who else? Gallic's. That was his big thing. Everywhere he went, he had a movie camera with him. He was always taking pictures of us, and then we'd have to take pictures of him."

"Everywhere?"

"I don't ever remember seeing him go anyplace without one."

"When you say 'without one,' you mean he had more than one?"

"He had two for sure that I knew of. Probably had another one."

"You ever see these movies?"

"Sure. Everytime we'd go out to his trailer, he'd show them."

"You see the one from Mexico?"

Janeski sighed and then nodded slowly. "Yeah. That one, too."

"Was that when things started to go bad between you and your wife?"

"Nah. That was just the lid. I mean, you stay away from your wife as long as I did after that trip, she got to figure something out. And what could I tell her—that I got the clap from some little whore, one that wasn't as tall as my own daughter? How was I supposed to tell her that? So I just stayed away from her. I didn't even kiss her until I was positive it was cured. I went to three different doctors, man, just to make sure. By that time, she didn't want me to kiss her no more. . . ."

"Listen, Richie, for the time being, let's forget about that part of it, okay?"

"That's about all there was to it anyway, man. You asked me why I would want to kill Gallic. I just told you why. But I'm telling you again I didn't."

"Okay, we'll let that go. But how many other movies did Gallic have like that one?"

"Like the one from Mexico?"

"Yes."

"A whole bunch, man. And he was in every one of them."

"Who took those? Did you?"

"No. That one from Mexico was the only one like that I ever had anything to do with."

"But he had a lot?"

"Yeah. I couldn't say how many, but a lot, that's for sure. You know, at first I used to get my jollies watching them. I mean, they're pretty funny, you know? And when you know the guy, they're even funnier. Maybe I'm nuts, but they were funny to me. At least until he got that one developed from Mexico. That's when it stopped being funny. I mean, I watched it, but then, sitting there, looking at myself and knowing what the result was, man, it was all I could do to keep from throwing up. And I remember thinking that was the first time I ever thought there was something really wrong with that stuff. And then I started looking at Gallic altogether different. Up until then, I don't know, it was like Gallic couldn't do anything wrong. Like whatever he did or whatever he wanted to do, that was okay with me. Up until that, you know, most of the things he wanted to do, hell, I thought it was all great."

"But that changed everything," Balzic said.

"Yeah. But it was too late then. My wife was already gone. The day she left, man, she said something that really pissed me off. I wanted to smack her for saying it. I didn't. But I wanted to. Now, I don't know. I think maybe she was right."

"What was that?"

"She hated Gallic. From the start. Couldn't stand the sight of him. And the day she left, she was almost out the door, she said, 'When you're around him, you act like he's your father.' It really pissed me. I really wanted to smack her for saying that, but all I did was tell her she didn't know what she was talking about."

"Now you figure she was right?"

"I don't know. She said I'd been looking for a father ever since my old man whacked me across the head. I couldn't see it. I mean, I hated that guy, so why would I be looking for somebody to take his place? But thinking about it all this time, I guess maybe I was. I used to ask myself why I buddied up with a couple guys that much older than me, and then I'd think back about it, about everything Gallic said—hell, everything he said to do, I did, just like a kid. Better than a kid. A kid'll give you some steam once in a while. Least mine used to. But I never got smart with Gallic. Even after my wife left, I still never got snotty with him. I just tried to stay away from him as much as I could. It worked for a while, but then, I don't know, I just started hanging around with him again. Just started the same old crap."

"The movies, too?"

"Huh-uh. No way. I mean pictures of us hunting and fishing, yeah. But not that other stuff. I wouldn't even sit still and watch that kind. At least not—"

"Not what?"

"Huh-uh, man. That's all I'm going to say." Janeski's expression and tone had changed abruptly the moment he'd said the word not, as though a circuit breaker had been overloaded and popped out, refusing to carry the current any farther. His gaze dropped to the floor and stayed there. His knee started bouncing again, and he pocketed the hanky he'd been squeezing since he'd cried. He started to knead his hands.

"You can't stop now, Richie."

"Who says?" Janeski said, eyes still downcast. "I spilled my guts enough. Bawling, Jesus . . ."

"I doubt this was the first time. Something tells me you cried a lot, those times you were laying in bed asking somebody to get it over with."

"So what if I did? Ain't I allowed?"

"Oh, I know you are. But something tells me you don't think you are."

Janeski closed his eyes and shook his head from side to side petulantly.

"Men are allowed to cry, you know," Balzic said.

"Yeah. Sure."

"They are. I never knew a man worth knowing who didn't cry once in a while. There's no shame in it. Only the guys who don't know they're men get nervous about it."

Janeski jumped up so suddenly he knocked his chair over backwards. "What the fuck are you—some kind of head doctor? What the fuck do you know about it?"

"I know a man when I see one."

"Yeah? You also know when you see one that ain't?"

"See one that ain't what?" Balzic asked softly.

"Ain't a man. Do you know when you see a man that ain't a man? Come on. I want to hear the answer to that one."

"Do you mean is there something that shows?"

"Yeah. Just what do you look for? The way he walks? If he walks like a broad—is that what you look for? 'Cause if it is, if that's what you look for, man, I'll give you a hint. You'll be wrong."

"How will I be wrong?"

"You'll be wrong, that's all." Janeski's tone took another turn. He jammed his hands in his pockets and shuffled obliquely away from Balzic.

"Yes, but in what way will I be wrong, Richie?"

"I don't know. You'll be wrong, that's all I know."

"I won't know if you don't tell me."

"Aw, go to the library, man. Go get yourself some books. You sound like a guy that reads books."

"Did you go to the library?"

"That's a laugh. Feature me in a library. What would I be doing there?"

"I don't know. Maybe you were reading about guys that aren't guys."

"That's a real laugh."

"Then how come you're not laughing?"

Janeski looked over his shoulder at Balzic. "Ah what is this, man? You think I did something, then take me wherever you take people that did something. Why don't you do that? Why don't you say something about letting me call a lawyer? Ain't that what you're supposed to do? Why don't you do that? You know what I think?"

"What?"

"I think you don't have the first idea who killed Gallic. And I think you got me and Peluzzi in here because somebody's looking to get himself a little front page. Some headlines."

"As a matter of fact, Richie, there are only a couple people who even know Gallic's dead. The newspaper sure doesn't. Not even the DA knows yet."

"Well what's it going to be then? We just going to stay here and talk until we fall down or what? I already told you I didn't do it. And I also already told you we weren't the last ones to see him."

"That's what you told me all right. What you haven't told me is who was."

"Some broad."

"Which broad?"

"I don't know. Never saw her before or since."

"You're leaving something out."

"No shit, Dick Tracy."

"Look, Richie. I wasn't just talking before when I said you and Peluzzi are up for this one. The DA doesn't know yet, but he's going to know pretty soon. And when he does, he's going to want some names. Because the DA is one of those people always looking to get himself some front page. And I'll tell you what, the fact that you two spent that last weekend with Gallic plus the fact that you told me in plain words that you wanted to kill Gallic, well, you figure it out."

"I also told you in plain words I didn't do it neither."

"Richie, if you walked into any jail, workhouse, reformatory, prison, or penitentiary, and you asked everybody in any one of them, or everybody in all of them, nine-hundred-ninety-nine out of a thousand are going to tell you they didn't do it. And they said it all along, right from the time they were arrested, right on through their arraignment, all the way through all their appeals. More than one died saying that. I'll spare you the sermon, but I'll tell you straight. You know something, you better tell me."

"Why? Why should I do that? Maybe it wouldn't be such a bad idea to let the state take care of me."

"Oh quit talking crap. You're so sorry for Richie Janeski you're starting to make me sick."

"Good. I'm glad somebody else is sick for a change."

"Knock that off. Tell me which broad."

"I told you I don't know. I wouldn't know her name if she walked in here right now."

"Then how do you expect me to believe there even was a broad? Where did you see her? When? How do you know she was the last to see Gallic?"

"She was, all right."

"That tells me nothing."

"Okay," Janeski said. "Okay. You want to know who she was? Then go find the movies. She'll be there, big as life.

Gallic made six or seven movies with her. And you know what the joke was? She didn't even know."

"The movies," Balzic said. "The movies. So that's why . . ."

"What?"

"Nothing. Just thinking out loud," Balzic said. "Okay, Richie, let's have the rest of it. All of it. And don't leave anything out."

"Why should I?"

"Change your attitude, goddammit. The game's over. I know you didn't kill Gallic. But there are still laws in this county about having movies like those, never mind being in them. That's one of the DA's favorite misdemeanors. You think so damn much of your kids, you better think how it's going to go for them if people in this town find out you're a movie star. 'Cause there's not a doubt in my mind those movies are still around. Somebody's been looking for them for three months."

Balzic stood up. "I'm going to make a phone call, but when I get back, you better have the rest of that weekend lined up for me. Minute by minute. Otherwise, you're going to wish the state *would* take care of you, as sick as you're going to be when your kids find out about this."

"Wait a minute!" Janeski cried out, but Balzic was out the door and hustling to a phone.

"Hey, Mario," Stramsky said, "Minyon called twice—"

"That's who I'm calling now," Balzic said, dialing.

"State police. Corporal Roman speaking."

"This is Mario Balzic. I want to talk to Minyon."

A click, then a pause. "Lieutenant Minyon."

"Minyon, this is Balzic—"

"Where the hell have you been, Balzic?"

"Never mind. Just go get a search warrant and get your people together. Go out to Galsam's Freezer Meats and do a job on that place."

"Oh really? So you've finally figured out whose side you're on."

"Don't get shitty, Minyon. Just do what I said."

"And just what is it I'm supposed to be looking for out there?"

"Movies."

"What?"

"You heard me. Seems Frank Gallic was a movie nut—among all the other kinds he was."

"Is this another one of your jokes, Balzic?"

"Listen, Minyon, if you don't want to trouble yourself, just say so. The fact is I'd rather go out there myself than have you go, but I'd be doing it alone. You have the people, and there's a business out there, plus two trailers, and at least three vehicles. It'd take me a week. But if you don't want to do it, just say the word."

"I'll do it—in return for a favor."

"I'm listening."

"I'd like you to locate a Richard Janeski and, let me see, an Axal Peluzzi. Your people know this town better than my people, and we've been looking since this afternoon and nobody knows anything."

"Sure," Balzic said. "I'll put it on the horn soon as I hang up. Is that all?"

"That's all. You're sure it's movies you want us to look for?"

"That's what I said. Should be a lot of them. But even a lot wouldn't take much space. They're probably in cans —hell, you know what movies look like."

"All right, Balzic. You'll let me know about Janeski and Peluzzi? I have an idea they'll be able to put this whole thing together."

"Maybe they will. I'll keep in touch." Balzic hung up and grinned at Stramsky. "The big man in the boy scout hat wants us to look for a couple guys named Janeski and Peluzzi. Seems he has an idea they know something."

"Oh yeah?" Stramsky said. "Did he have any clues for us to go on?"

"No. We're supposed to tough it out ourselves. But the

big man did admit we know this town better than he does."

"Imagine that," Stramsky said. "Next thing you know he'll be saying kolbassi don't taste too bad."

"Ah, I think I better go easy on friend Minyon. He doesn't have the first idea what I just let him in for. Maybe I should've told him to take along a couple straitjackets."

"Who for?"

"Mickey Samarra. And his sister. I'll tell you, if I was them, somebody would have to put me in a coat."

Stramsky looked puzzled, but Balzic did not bother to explain. Instead, he went back to the cubicle where Axal Peluzzi sat staring at the wall and chewing on a hangnail.

Balzic didn't take off his coat and he didn't sit. He pulled up the other chair and put his foot on it and leaned on his knee.

"All right, Peluzzi," he said, "let's have the rest of that weekend."

"Balzic, why don't you go to hell?"

"Not just yet. Someday maybe. But when I get there, you'll be cleaning the crapper."

"Oh, that's funny."

"I thought so. But it's not as funny as you in the movies."

"Me in the what?" Peluzzi stopped chewing his hangnail.

"The movies. You know—motion pictures. I hear you're almost a star. You're not as big on the marquee as your buddy Gallic was, but you're still pretty big. How's it feel to be almost a star?"

"I don't know what the fuck you're talking about."

"You don't know about taking movies with Gallic? You don't know about Gallic taking movies of you and Janeski? You don't know anything about that?"

"I ain't been to a movie in over a year."

"What's that have to do with anything? Or are you trying to tell me the last time you were at the movies cured you? Is that it?"

"You're not making sense, Balzic."

"You're the one not making sense. I know all about the movies. You and Janeski and Gallic. Frank Gallic, the producer, the director, the man who liked to look at himself. You three fishing. First Gallic takes some shots of you or Janeski hauling in a big one. Couple all-American boys in their fight against nature. Then later on you take a couple shots of Gallic making coffee around the campfire. Tranquil little scene. The hungry heroes settle down to enjoy their catch. How am I doing so far, Peluzzi?"

"So what's wrong with that? So we took some movies. So what?"

"Not a thing. Movie camera's a great invention. Homemade history, somebody said once. You have a picnic, somebody has a camera, and there you are, recorded for all time with your face in a watermelon."

"So?"

"So how about the other kind, that other kind of picnic?"

"What other kind?"

"You know. You and Janeski and Gallic in Mexico, say. You been out hunting something ferocious, and after the hunt, the heroes have a little fun. They find themselves a couple little girls and they all retreat to the hotel for a little good, clean fun. How about that?"

Peluzzi put another cigarette in his mouth and fumbled for a match.

"You didn't have a light before, Peluzzi, remember?"

"So I didn't."

Balzic lit Peluzzi's cigarette and waited. "Well?"

"So what's the big deal? So we got some broads in a room and we took some pictures. Nobody twisted their arms. They got paid. Cost me a small bundle to get rid of what they gave me, so who really came up short? Besides, that don't mean I had anything to do with killing Gallic."

"So you haven't forgotten that?"

"Comedian. How'm I supposed to forget that? I'm still here, ain't I?"

"The time you been having with your memory, Peluzzi, it's a small miracle you remember anything. So maybe we ought to go back over some things. You do remember Gallic having a movie camera, and you do remember the three of you taking turns with that camera, is that right?"

"I remember that, yeah."

"You also remember one movie in particular from Mexico, right?"

"Not so clear, but I remember it."

"Well, suppose you try to remember how many other movies there were like that one."

"I don't remember any more like that one."

"You don't remember being in any more like that one, or you don't remember any more like that one—which?"

"I was only in Mexico once, so how many could there be?"

"Any from Canada like that? From Alaska? Or how about from right here in Rocksburg?"

Peluzzi said nothing.

"Come off it, Peluzzi. I know there were lots. That's Janeski's word. Lots. Lots of movies like that one. Gallic was in most of them. But let's say that was the only one like that you were in. You're still in trouble, 'cause the DA has a special bitch about movies like that. He just loves to tell old ladies how much he's doing to fight corruption and moral decay."

Peluzzi canted his head and squinted through the smoke. "Little while ago you were telling me I was up for Gallic's murder. Now you're just talking about that movie."

"That's right. Right now, that's all I'm talking about."

"Well, which is it, Balzic? I mean, so the DA got a hard on for skin pictures. So what? The most I could get out of that is a couple hundred bucks' fine and maybe thirty days —if I had a dumb lawyer."

"That's right."

"So—so are you still talking about the same thing?"

"The same, but not exactly the same. The way I figure it, Peluzzi, somebody was in some of Gallic's movies and didn't know about it. You knew about it, and Janeski knew, 'cause Gallic showed them to you. You sat around, had a few drinks, and had some laughs. And there were some broads, not only in Mexico and Canada, but from around here, they knew about it, too. Maybe they even had a few laughs themselves. But there was somebody who was in them who not only didn't know she was in them, but who when she found out didn't think they were the least bit funny. In fact, they made her about as mad as anybody gets."

Peluzzi continued to smoke and squint at Balzic.

"What I'm trying to say, Peluzzi, is she thought she knew Gallic pretty good. And then one night she found out she didn't know him half as good as she thought."

"So?"

"Let me put it to you this way. If she didn't know him half as good as she thought, then the chances are pretty good other people didn't know Gallic as good as they thought, 'cause this female is pretty shrewd. And she knew Gallic a lot better than a lot of other people who'd been around him a lot longer than she had. But not good enough."

"What's all this have to do with me?"

"What I'm getting at is maybe you didn't know Gallic anywhere near as good as you thought you did. I mean, Janeski thought Gallic was something extra special for a long time, and then all of a sudden, he thinks maybe he should've killed him. Yeah. Imagine that, Peluzzi. That's something, isn't it? I mean, here's a guy who knows another guy as good as Janeski knew Gallic, and not only knows him but respects him. Admires him. Does everything the guy says to do, and never gives him an argument about it. Then all of a sudden he's saying he not only wanted to kill him, but he should have. Now, that's a helluva thing to say, especially to a cop, and especially not ten minutes after he finds out that other guy is dead. Murdered. And the cop is trying to find out who killed that other guy? Don't you think that's a helluva thing to say?"

"Why don't you ask Janeski? He's the one said it, not me."

"I already have. Now I'm asking you. How good did you know Gallic?"

"I knew him."

"How long?"

"Ten years. Maybe longer."

"And you went hunting with him, fishing with him, drinking with him. You took turns taking movies of one another —all kinds of movies, Peluzzi. And I probably wouldn't be far wrong to say you probably slept with him."

Peluzzi's head snapped up. "What do you mean by that?"

"You know. You camped out together, right? So you had to be pretty close. Those campers aren't too big. Tents —tents are pretty small things."

"His camper was big."

"I've seen his camper, Peluzzi. It isn't anything out of the ordinary. It's no bigger than most campers that fit on the back of a pickup truck. And I've been inside them. I know how big they are."

Peluzzi started to say something and then apparently changed his mind.

"Look at it this way, Peluzzi. There's a guy who knew Gallic for years—twenty-seven to be exact—and you'd think he'd be the one guy to know Gallic better than anybody, but I'll bet you a hundred bucks against a dime, he will be the most surprised guy in the world when he finds out Gallic owned a movie camera, never mind what kind of pictures he took. As far as that goes, all he knew was Gallic used to bring some real skags back to his trailer, and all he was worried about was that Gallic might catch something. But when Gallic did catch something that time in Mexico, he didn't know about that."

"He must not've known him too good."

"Oh, he thought he did. He thought he knew him real

good. And not only that, he thinks he knows you real good too. The fact is, he told me he knew you since you were a kid, and he said you aren't a very good person. Those were his exact words. You aren't a good person. You know who I'm talking about?"

"Samarra. Who else?"

"That's right. And he doesn't like you even a little bit. 'Cause he didn't like what you and Janeski did to Gallic when you were out together."

"What *we* did to Gallic? Samarra's head is bent, that's what's wrong with him. I never did nothing to Gallic. Anything Gallic did, it was 'cause he wanted to do it. I never put no ideas in his head. Christ, I knew Samarra was dumb, but that takes it all, brother—what we did to Gallic. Shit."

"Yeah, no doubt about it. Mickey Samarra's a little slow. But he's also, uh, one of the strongest guys I've ever known. Even when he was a kid, nobody would fool with him. And he never wanted to hurt anybody. But just fooling around with other kids, he'd hurt them. You remember that. Who didn't know that about him? Did you ever look at his hands? I mean, did you ever take a good look at them?"

"Why should I? I look funny for hands or something?"

"That guy, short as he is, what a pair of hands he's got. And all he does all day is throw that beef around."

"So he ought to be in a circus. So what's your point?"

"Simple point, Peluzzi. I'm surprised you haven't thought of it yourself. I mean, you said yourself a little while ago, even if the DA does have a hard on against skin pictures, the most you could get is a fine and maybe thirty days. You get a half-decent lawyer, you won't even get that. But just what do you think Mickey Samarra's going to want to do when he finds out about those movies?"

"What are you trying to do, Balzic? That doesn't have nothing to do with me. I wasn't the one with his sister in those movies. That was Gallic. And he's dead, right?"

"So you knew it was Tina Samarra?"

"Sure I knew. What am I—blind?"

"Of course she wasn't the only one."

"Are you kidding? She was just the last."

"What puzzles me is how he managed to bring it off without her knowing about it."

"Simple. He had a camera set up in a closet inside the bathroom. He had a little hole in the wall into the bedroom. Then when he'd get the broad into bed, he'd say he had to go take a shower. He'd tell them he didn't like to make love dirty. He wanted to be clean, and that's when he'd start the camera. When he came out of the shower."

"So most of them never knew?"

"How could they? He'd have the air-conditioner on plus the stereo, so they couldn't hear the camera going."

"But he never said who they were, did he? Especially not Mickey's sister."

"No."

"And naturally you never let on you knew, about her, I mean."

"Why should I? But he knew I knew. 'Cause he used to get a special laugh about her. He used to say, 'This one's fucking wacky. She loves me.' That's what he used to say about her. But I knew all right."

"So there was really only one time and one way she could've found out," Balzic said. "I mean, if nobody told her . . ."

"You're doing the talking."

"It's impossible for me to believe she stumbled on it before. That would have been the end of her and Gallic. Besides, she wasn't living there then."

Peluzzi said nothing.

"So the only time was when she did. Which brings us back to that weekend. You and Janeski and Gallic fishing and drinking beer, you said. That and nothing else."

Peluzzi crushed out his cigarette and said, "I'm tired talking."

"Are you now? Then maybe you better listen better, Peluzzi. 'Cause the way I see it, you got one chance of staying alive once Mickey Samarra finds out about those movies. And that one chance is I give you a long head start and you just disappear. Otherwise, Mickey Samarra'll tear you apart. He'll get those mitts of his on you and, strong as you are, Peluzzi, you won't have a chance. And you better listen good to this part: I'm not going to stop him, and you said yourself the most you could get is thirty days.

"After that, you'd have to come out, and you're dago enough to know what an old-school dago like him thinks about somebody messing with his sister. Especially messing with her like that. And what will really make it worse for you is that Gallic is already dead. Which means, in case you haven't figured that out, is that Samarra won't have Gallic to kill. But he's going to want to kill somebody.

"And here's one more thing for you to think about before you tell me you're tired talking: the state police are out there right now looking for those movies. In other words, friend, you don't have too much time. Because, hell, let's be practical. How long do you think it would be before you came to trial? Couple of months? What are you going to do in the meantime—just keep on collecting checks and walking around like nothing happened? Better think again, Peluzzi, 'cause right now I'm the only person between you and Mickey Samarra, and unless you tell me the rest of what happened that weekend, I'm just going to open that door and let you walk on out of here. How'd you like that?

"'Cause Mickey won't care if he gets locked up for a hundred years once he finds out about those movies. His life will be over as far as he's concerned. The shame will be a thousand times worse than getting locked up. And the only thing that will make that shame easier for him to live with is the satisfaction that he killed you."

"Why the fuck do you keep saying me? Goddammit, Janeski was in on it, too! I wasn't the only one. Janeski was there too! I wasn't the only one Gallic queered!"

"The only one he what?"

"You heard me." Peluzzi averted his eyes. "And if you

think you're going to get me to say any more than that,
you're crazy."

"So that was it," Balzic said. "So that's what happened.
Your hero, Janeski's hero, the big-game hunter—turns out he
was queer. I'll be damned. He must've hid it pretty good
all those years."

"Not so good," Peluzzi said, eyes still downcast. "Not
when I think back about it."

"How so?"

"Ah, he was always goosing somebody. You'd walk by
him, he'd make a grab for your crotch. Stuff like that."

"But lots of other guys do that, right? So you never gave
it a second thought. But something must've made you think
about it."

"There was something, all right. That time in Mexico he
tried to get those two whores to go down on each other.
But they wouldn't go for it. Maybe they didn't understand
him. But he sure tried."

"And he must've tried with others. And succeeded."

"Yeah, he had a couple reels like that. He really got a boot
in the ass out of watching them."

"So when it happened at Tionesta, it surprised you, but
not really, is that it?"

"The thing was, we were all pretty drunk, and I remember
him saying we ought to circle jerk—you know how when
you was a kid—well, not you, I guess. Nah, you wouldn't of
gone for that kind of shit. But some kids'll get in a circle
and see how far they can leak, that's how it starts. Then the
next thing would be to see who could beat off and come the
fastest. Well, that's what Gallic thought up. He said we
should all throw five bucks in and whoever comes first gets
the fifteen. Like I said, we were all pretty drunked up anyway, so we went for it. One thing led to another, and the
next thing I know, Gallic's down on me."

"On Janeski too?"

"Yeah, him too. So don't just be hollering at me and telling me what Samarra's going to be doing to me."

"All right, I won't. But then what happened—you start to sober up?"

Peluzzi sighed. "What do you think? Course we started to sober up. That's a long drive back from there. And Gallic was really starting to sweat it. He wouldn't shut up talking about it. He kept saying how lots of guys do that. Real guys, he kept saying, not just them swishers you see in some bars. Said it would probably never happen again in a million years. . . ."

"But he could tell you two weren't buying it."

"It wasn't too hard. I felt pretty shitty myself, so I just kept on drinking. But Janeski, hell, he wouldn't say nothing. All the way back, he didn't say five words."

"Which left only one thing for Gallic to do, right? I mean, if he's still going to be the big man?"

"What else?"

"What I can't figure is how he managed to get Tina out there and get you two out there as well."

"Tell you the truth, I don't know myself how he swung that. All I know is, when he dropped us off at my place, he got us to promise him we'd be there. Christ, he was pathetic. I never saw him like that before. He was practically begging us."

"Did you know it was going to be Tina?"

"He didn't say who. He just said he'd have this broad there and she'd go for anything. He guaranteed it. All we had to do was give him time to get her warmed up and get some booze in her."

"What time was all this?"

"I'm not sure. He must've dropped us off about nine at my place. Then he said to give him a couple hours. So it was probably eleven, eleven-thirty when I got there."

"Janeski was there, too?"

"He showed about five minutes after I did. For a while, he didn't want to get out of his car. He just sat there looking, looking like I don't know what. Tell you the truth, I was a little bit scared of the way he looked."

"Did you talk to him? I mean, did you try to talk him into going inside?"

"No. I tried to tell him to forget it, that's all. He just looked at me. But Gallic's the one that talked him into going in. He came out of the trailer bare ass and he said what the fuck are we waiting for."

"So you went in?"

"Not right away. It took him a couple minutes to convince Janeski. But then we went in. But we didn't stay too goddamn long."

"As soon as Tina find out, it was all over, right?"

"You better believe it was all over. I never seen a broad that mad in my life. Nobody. Never that mad. So if you can't figure out by now who killed him, Balzic, you're some kind of dumb."

"Oh, I figured that out a while ago. Soon as I found out about the movies. I just wanted to know why." Balzic went to the door. "Okay, Peluzzi, all you have to decide is whether you want to chance walking around or whether you want to be locked up until the trial. You think it over."

"Hey! There ain't nothing to think over. You lock me up, man. And then you make sure I get out of this town."

"Don't worry about that. I'll make sure. Just you make sure you don't do anything stupid while you're waiting for the trial."

"I ain't going to do nothing stupid."

"Don't be so sure. You got a history of it," Balzic said, leaving the cubicle and closing the door behind him.

He went out into the squad room and asked Stramsky if there had been any word from Minyon.

"Not yet," Stramsky said.

"Okay. Then put Peluzzi downstairs. He's going to be with us for a while. Make sure he's clean."

Stramsky nodded and got the necessary forms and started filling them in.

Balzic went on to the cubicle where Janeski waited, raw-eyed and cracking his knuckles.

"Okay, Richie," Balzic said, "Peluzzi gave me most of it. Now I want to hear it from you."

"He tell you everything?"

"If by everything you mean the part about Gallic queering you, yeah."

"Oh, Jesus," Janeski said, covering his ears with his hands, his eyes flying desperately.

"Come on, Janeski, get yourself together. Give me some times and the travel arrangements. Peluzzi says Gallic dropped you two off at Peluzzi's place about nine, is that right?"

Janeski dropped his hands to his sides and turned his back to Balzic. "Yeah," he said, his voice breaking, just on the edge of a sob. "It was about then. Little after maybe."

"And Gallic got you two to promise him you'd meet him at his place a couple hours later?"

"Yeah."

"You got there around eleven-thirty?"

"Yeah."

"Peluzzi says you didn't want to go in, is that right?"

"That's right. I didn't even know what I was doing out there with that queer bastard."

"But you finally went in after Gallic came out and talked you into it, right?"

"Yeah. I did. Peluzzi too."

"What I can't figure out is why you even showed up."

Janeski shook his head violently. "I don't know. Honest to God, I thought about it a thousand times. And I still don't know. Sometimes I think I went out there to kill him. At least that's what I like to think I was doing there."

"Did you take something with you? A pistol? Knife?"

"I had my twenty-two with me. In the glove compartment."

"But you didn't take it in."

"No. That's when I knew I didn't have no balls left. I just went on in. Just like I didn't have any brains either. . . ."

"How long were you three in there before she found out what was going on?"

"Couldn't have been more than a couple minutes. Wasn't too damn long, I know that."

"Where was she when you first went in?"

"I don't know. She must've been in the bedroom."

"What made her come out? Did Gallic call her?"

"I don't know. But Gallic didn't call her. He was telling me and Peluzzi to get undressed. I was just standing there, trying to figure out why he was whispering. I mean, if it was the kind of broad he said was going to be there, what was he trying to hide? So I didn't even start to take my clothes off. But Peluzzi, he started to take his pants off, and he was still half shot, and he couldn't get them off without taking his shoes off. So he bent over to take his shoes off and he lost his balance and started hobbling around and knocked over a lamp. That was when she came out."

"Did you recognize her?"

"I told you before. I recognized her from the movies. She was in five or six of them. I spotted her from them."

"But you didn't know her?"

"No. Not then."

"When did you find out who she was?"

"Peluzzi told me."

"When was this?"

"Couple months later. He called me up and asked me if I wanted to go hunting with him. I said if it was with Gallic, forget it. But he said it would be just me and him, so I went."

"And then you found out it was Mickey Samarra's sister."

"Yeah."

"So why'd you lie about it before?"

Janeski groaned. "Man, I've been trying to forget this whole goddamn mess. You didn't get out of me what Gallic did. You got that out of Peluzzi, remember?"

"I remember very clearly," Balzic said. "So what did you think about after you found out who she was?"

"I told you. I just wanted to get the whole load of crap out of my head."

"But you couldn't. Not with those movies still around."

"What do you think? I busted my head trying to figure that out. Once I even tried to make a deal with some guy who was supposed to be a pro. A burglar. From Pittsburgh. But he wanted something out of this world. Five bills. Plus another bill for every time it took him past three times. I didn't have that kind of money."

"So you just went along, not doing much of anything. What were you hoping for?"

"Hoping. That's all I was doing. Hoping everything would just go away. Then Peluzzi calls me up and tells me she's back living out there, so we know what she's looking for."

"But you still didn't do anything?"

"What was I supposed to do? Go ask her if she wanted some help? If you'd've seen her that night when she walked out and saw Peluzzi trying to get his pants off, you wouldn't be so goddamn anxious to get close to her either."

"So then why hang around? You had money. A car. You weren't strapped in here like Peluzzi. He's got people all over town looking for him with their hands out. But you could've left any time."

"Maybe I wanted to get it over with. Maybe I figured with Gallic gone all I had to do to get myself straightened out was stay away from Peluzzi. Then . . . well, if I went someplace, that'd mean I'd never get to see my kids."

"You knew Gallic was gone?"

"Sure I knew. Nobody saw him. What I figured was it got him worse than it got either Peluzzi or me, so he just cut out. I'll tell you what, when that broad came out and saw us three standing there, man, all I was thinking about was getting the hell out of there as fast as I could move. And I figured Peluzzi and Gallic would be doing the same thing."

"You didn't stay to see if they did?"

"Hell, no. I got that car in gear and floored it. I must've laid a strip of rubber fifty yards long. Then later on, when

Peluzzi called me, I figured he got out, so Gallic must've got out too. I'll tell you the truth, I never even thought for a second she'd kill him."

"You must not have been worrying too much about those movies."

"Well, when I thought about it awhile, I figured, so what if she finds them? What's she going to do with them—show them down the Roxian?"

"Didn't you ever think about her brother?"

"He's a jerk. Besides, there again, what was she going to do? I mean, feature it. She calls him in and says, pull up a chair, brother, I got some really good movies I want you to see? Are you kidding? Man, the way I figured it, the best thing that could happen was for her to find them."

"Too bad. 'Cause now you're staring at the worst thing. Her brother—that *jerk*—is going to find out about them pretty soon. He's going to know about everything pretty soon," Balzic said. "I'll tell you what. I'll give you the same choice I gave Peluzzi."

"What's that?"

"You can walk out and take your chances with her brother or you can let me lock you up until the trial. After which I guarantee her brother won't know which way you went or how you were traveling."

Janeski thought about that a minute. "So it still winds up I don't even get to see my kids once a week."

"I'm not going to tell you you should've thought of that before."

"Thanks for nothing. Jesus . . ."

"So what's it going to be? You want to walk, or you want a cell?"

"What do you think?" Janeski said. "Just tell me one thing. How much of this you think'll come out at the trial?"

"If I was her lawyer, I'd turn over every rock there was. You figure it out."

"So my family's going to find out anyway."

Balzic shrugged.

"Jesus," Janeski said. "What do you guarantee them?"

"If you got any money saved, you'd be smart to get them out of here. One of you has to have some relatives someplace. Course, in something like this, friends would probably be better than relatives. If you want me to talk to her for you, I will. And if you're short, I'll see what I can do about getting you a loan. Beyond that, there isn't much I can do. Which is a helluva lot, I might add. But there's one thing nobody could do, and that's stop people from talking."

Janeski hung his head and his shoulders started to jerk.

"Think it over, Richie. Take your time. You'll be here for a while."

Balzic stepped out of the cubicle and went over to Stramsky. "Put Janeski downstairs, Vic."

While Stramsky was doing the paperwork, Balzic took everything from Janeski which he could possibly use to commit suicide, including the plastic buttons off Janeski's back pockets.

"What're you doing that for?" Janeski asked.

"You'd be surprised the edge you can put on plastic if you rub it on cement long enough. It won't cut paper, but it'll cut flesh. And I don't want you doing anything dumb, 'cause if we get lucky, this thing can be hushed up pretty good."

Janeski signed for his personal effects and followed Stramsky downstairs.

In a minute Stramsky was back. "Christ," he said, "you ought to hear the names they're calling one another. I thought I heard them all."

"Naturally," Balzic said. "That's what they been doing all their lives, even when nothing was wrong. Now that something is wrong?" He shrugged and started for the door. "I'm going out to see what Minyon came up with, Vic. Don't know how long I'll be, so if Ruth calls, give her the good news. But gently."

Balzic was in no hurry to get out to Galsam's Freezer Meats. Of all the people and things to be found there, he could think of none pleasant. Only the whereabouts of the movies still piqued his curiosity, and he knew that once they were found, all that followed would be more or less routine. No matter what the papers did with this when they found out about it, no matter how bizarre or grisly they tried to make it, it was downhill as far as he was concerned.

He parked beside the three state police cruisers and sat a moment watching the shadows moving inside Frank Gallic's trailer, wondering how Mickey and Tina were reacting to it. He imagined a look of betrayal on Mickey's face, and he did not want to confront him. There was no telling in whose direction Mickey would want to lash out.

Balzic got out of his car finally after smoking a cigarette down until he could feel the heat from the ash on his fingers. When he knew he could procrastinate no longer, he went inside and stood just inside the door and watched Minyon's men. They were thorough and efficient, but because they were still in the process of being thorough and efficient, Balzic knew they hadn't found the movies.

Minyon appeared then from the rear of the trailer, probably from the bedroom, and it was only when Minyon stopped to speak to him that Balzic noticed Tina and Mickey. They were sitting in the kitchen, their bodies obscured by the bottom half of a room divider, Mickey's eyes going from one trooper to another as they searched, Tina's eyes fixed on the divider, her head seemingly suspended in a cloud of her own cigarette smoke.

"You sure it's movies we're supposed to be looking for?" Minyon whispered, leaning close to Balzic.

Balzic nodded. "Did you tell them what you were looking for?"

"No. I just let them read the search warrant. Her, rather. He didn't want to look at it. He took her word for it. But we sure as hell haven't found anything that even looks like a movie yet. Hell, we haven't even found any snapshots."

"Well, how about doing me a favor and getting him out of here. I want to talk to her, and I don't want him to hear any of it."

"Balzic, before I go doing you any more favors, I'd like to know what the hell this is all about."

"You get him out of here and you can listen while I talk to her. You'll figure it out as I go along. I don't feel like going through it with you and then going through it with her all over again. I've already gone through it enough as it is. I just went through the whole thing with Janeski and Peluzzi."

"You found them?"

"Sure I found them. You said yourself we know this town better than you do. It wasn't any big thing. Now how about it?"

Minyon sighed irritably. "All right. I'll do it your way, but it better be good."

"It will be, don't worry."

Minyon called one of the troopers over and told him to take Mickey Samarra out on the pretense of looking around the other trailer.

Mickey passed Balzic without a word. It was as though he did not recognize Balzic, or as though he could not associate a name with Balzic's face. The look of betrayal Balzic had anticipated was not there; rather, it seemed to Balzic that Mickey had discovered himself engulfed by some totally foreign atmosphere and could not guess why he was still able to survive.

Balzic stepped beyond the divider and into the kitchen area. He drew up a chair and, nodding to Tina, sat opposite her. She glanced at him indifferently, then crushed out her cigarette and in the same motion took another from her pack and lit it.

If she was disturbed because of the invasion of all these men—there were four troopers still searching in addition to Minyon and Balzic—she showed it only by seeming to draw more deeply into herself.

"Tina," Balzic began, "I think now's the time you tell me what you said you were going to when you got ready."

"I don't remember telling you anything like that."

"You did. Outside the lieutenant's office. When he had

Mickey with him, you said you were going to tell me some things when you got ready. I think now's the time."

"You would."

"Tina, I'll put it straight on the line. I know you killed Gallic. I know why. The only things I don't know are how and when."

Minyon's face showed infinitely greater surprise than did Tina's. She looked squarely at Balzic and said, "If you know that, then what difference does it make how or when."

"I suppose how doesn't really make that much difference. But when might make a difference. For your sake, it might make a helluva difference how long you waited to kill him."

"What difference does it make how long you wait before you butcher a pig? A pig is only fit for butchering. Sooner or later, that's all it's good for. When only makes a difference if you're going to sell it."

"It might make a tremendous difference at your trial. I know you're going to find this hard to believe, but I really don't want to see you pay any more for this than you absolutely have to."

"You're right. I find it very hard to believe."

"Then you're just going to have to take my word for it."

"I don't take any man's word for anything."

"I can understand that, but, uh, you're going to have to take mine."

"Why should I? You come in here after these goons come in and start tearing the place apart and you say you know I did this or that—you give me one reason why I should take your word for the time of day. I don't think you know anything."

"Well, I do. Maybe not the same things you know, but I do. And it would be a lot easier for everybody if you'd be more co-operative."

"A lot easier for everybody," Tina said, her face twisting in contempt. "All you have to do is co-operate . . . what that means is all I have to do is what you want me to do. You make me sick."

"Tina, I'm not Gallic, but—"

"Nobody's Gallic. Gallic isn't. Gallic never was. Just what he made me. Just what he tried to make me."

"—I started to say I'm not Gallic, and I'm not trying to get you to co-operate for my benefit, but for yours."

"Are you now? Funny. Seems I've heard that line a few times before. What's good for you is going to make me feel good, too. Isn't that the way it goes? All I have to do to feel good is make you feel good. No matter what. Don't you bastards ever think up anything new?"

"I guess I have to get at it from a different way—"

"Go all the ways you want. Fly around the moon if that gets it for you. Just get it. Get what you want. The hell with what anybody else wants. The hell with what I want."

"I know you don't believe me, Tina, but I have to admit in one sense you're right. I have to get it—the 'it' in this case being the truth—one way or another. So I guess it doesn't really matter whether you think I'm doing you a favor or not. Not in the long run."

"Balzic," Minyon interrupted, "will you quit talking in circles? Say what you have to say."

"There's a big man for you," Tina said. "Don't waste time. Don't find out anything. Don't see what might happen. Demand. Just demand. And you expect me to think you're any different."

Balzic lit a cigarette and thought a moment. "Okay. So here it is. To satisfy you both." He paused to look up at Minyon, a look as full of irritation and contempt as he could make it. "Gallic and Janeski and Peluzzi went fishing on a Friday fifteen months ago. The following Sunday they came back. Gallic dropped the other two off at Peluzzi's house and picked up Tina here. You were living in your parents' house then, the one in Norwood. That was around nine-thirty.

"Gallic brought you out here. I'm not sure how much trouble he had getting you out here, but whether you wanted to come out or not, pretty soon you got the impression something was really bothering him. You probably didn't ask him about it, and he sure as hell didn't say what it was, but there was no mistaking that something was on his mind.

"I, uh, hesitate to bring it up—what was on his mind, I mean—but for the lieutenant's benefit, Tina, I guess I have to. And I guess there's no way to say it but to just say it." Balzic stopped and looked at Minyon. "Gallic queered the other two."

Tina didn't blink, but Minyon's jaw dropped.

"Anyway," Balzic went on, "Gallic had to do something to prove to the other two that he was still all man, so before he went to get you, Tina, he got the other two to agree to come out here.

"About eleven-thirty, eleven thirty-five, after you and Gallic had had a few drinks and spent some time back there," Balzic said, nodding toward the bedroom, "you probably dozed off. You thought maybe you heard a car pull in, maybe two. You weren't sure. But then you noticed that Gallic wasn't beside you, and then you heard something. Voices maybe or somebody stumbling. Then you heard a lamp get knocked over. Am I right so far?"

Tina said nothing.

"Okay, so you got up and you came out and you saw Gallic, naked, with the other two. Janeski was just standing there, but Peluzzi was taking his pants off. It probably took you a couple seconds to figure it out, 'cause I'm sure at first you didn't want to believe it. But then you finally had to believe it.

"You scared Janeski so much, he took off in such a hurry he never found out until a month or so later whether Peluzzi even got out of here. But Peluzzi did manage to get out, so that left just you and Gallic. You and him, the guy you were getting ready to marry. That must have been a helluva moment, especially with him trying to tell you it wasn't what it looked like. From what I hear, he was a very persuasive guy. And something tells me he almost convinced you. How am I doing so far?"

Tina exhaled some smoke. She started to speak, then took another drag on her cigarette, and lapsed once again behind her mask.

"That's all right, Tina. You don't have to say anything," Balzic said. "Not yet anyway. So let me pick it up from there. Gallic was still talking, still trying to tell you you had it all wrong. You knew better, but you were probably starting to cool down anyway. In spite of yourself. Probably at that point all you were doing was berating yourself for being so stupid about him. Or so blind.

"But feeling stupid about him or blind or whatever didn't change how dirty you must have felt. Knowing you and your brother, your family as long as I have, I'd say you probably felt as dirty as you'd ever felt in your life. So the natural thing to do when you feel that way is to want to get clean. And that's when you went into the bathroom. And that's the part I can't exactly puzzle out. All I can do is make a guess, because Gallic would've shut that thing off long before, wouldn't he? So you couldn't have heard it."

"What thing?" Minyon asked.

"The camera. The one that took the movies your people are looking for. Gallic had it set up in the bathroom, focused into the bedroom so he could, uh, have a record of himself as a lover."

Tina shuddered then, an involuntary spasm that began in her hips and ended in a catch of breath.

"What it was," Balzic said to Minyon, "from what I can put together, is the guy needed a whole lot of proof. A sad thing, but there it is . . . but to get back to you, Tina, what I figure is you found it because you were probably looking for a clean towel or a clean washcloth or a fresh bar of soap. I mean, if you really wanted to get clean, as dirty as you felt, you wouldn't want to do it with Gallic's soap or washcloth or towel. Because he'd already taken a shower. That was when he'd turned on the camera. So that was how you found it, right? When you were looking for a clean washcloth or new soap?"

Tina continued to smoke, taking deep drags, blowing out the smoke in heavy breaths, her face as controlled as ever.

"So there was nothing left then," Balzic said. "Nothing at all. And only one way to get clean.

"What I figure is you came out to the kitchen for a knife, most likely, and then you went back into the bathroom, called him in, and told him to explain it. Maybe you didn't even ask for an explanation. And, uh, I'm really guessing now, but something tells me you had the presence of mind to make sure he'd fall into the bathtub."

Tina nodded then, the faintest suggestion of a nod, and she looked at Balzic as though, however grudgingly, she had to admit that a man was giving her credit for something and should be thanked for it. But she said nothing.

"Afterwards," Balzic said, "well, I see no reason to go into the rest of what you did. We all know that. I'm curious about one thing though, only because Mickey told me you never went near Gallic's truck. You used his truck, didn't you, to take the pieces out and bury them?"

"Mickey," Tina said. "Dumb Mickey . . ."

"The question still remains, how long between the time you found the camera and the time you killed him?"

"Not long," she said evenly. "When a pig's time comes, it comes."

"Okay, I'm not going to pester you about that. I'll leave it for your lawyer to convince you it's important. And I guess that leaves only the movies."

"If you find any," Tina said.

"How many have you found?"

"I didn't count them. I just burned them."

"Is that why you came back from Toledo?"

"You know the answer to that."

"You mean you didn't think there might be more until you'd been away for a whole year?"

"For a year I didn't want to think about anything. Then, well, I thought of it."

"Where did you look?"

"Everywhere but the right place until you showed up. Then when you came out asking questions—well, where do you look for shit?"

"In the toilet?"

"The only place I didn't look before. They were in plastic bags in the tank. That's the only good thing I can say for him. Even he knew where they belonged."

"Well," Balzic said, clearing his throat, "unless your people come up with some more, Lieutenant, we've got a problem."

"Such as what? What do we need them for? She just confessed. What more do we need?" Minyon said.

"Her confession here, just now, won't even satisfy the prosecuting attorney. And it damn sure isn't going to satisfy the lawyer that defends her."

"Since when is that our problem?"

"It's always been our problem, the way I figure it," Balzic said. "Or I guess I should say, I've always figured it was part of my problem. You can figure it any way you want."

"I figure it's her lawyer's problem," Minyon said.

"Yeah, I thought you would. But do me—and yourself— one more favor. After you get her booked and locked up, don't bother her until she has a lawyer with her, okay?"

"I don't need anybody's protection," Tina said. "I know what I did. And I'm not ashamed to say I did it. I'm not even ashamed of something else I did. Something you don't know about." She stood abruptly and went to a drawer near the sink.

Minyon lurched after her, but she stopped him with a laugh. "What do you think I'm going to do, big man? I just want you to see something."

She reached into the drawer where the silverware was and lifted a plastic tray and pulled out a square, flat object and tossed it on the table in front of Balzic. It took Balzic a long moment to understand what it was, and only when he made the association with others he had seen like it did it occur to him. It was a tattoo of the American flag with the words "Death Before Dishonor" below it. He had seen dozens like it when he had been in the Marines.

"That's all that's left of him," Tina said, "and if he hadn't taught me, I wouldn't've known how to do it."

Balzic felt something start to rise in his throat, swallowed once, and stood. "God, Tina, I'm—I'm sorry." He started for the door of the trailer.

"I don't need any goddamn apology from you," she called after him. "I'm not sorry. Who the hell are you to be sorry for me?"

Balzic did not turn around. Once in the car, he rolled down all the windows, and wheeled out of the parking lot, driving faster than he'd driven since he first got his license, hoping the wind screaming through the car and battering his face would somehow ease the sickness he felt.

After twenty minutes of wild driving, Balzic calmed himself. He had to talk out loud to succeed, but he did, and then he thought he should find Mo Valcanas. He found him in the lounge at the Rocksburg Bowling Alleys.

A saucer-eyed blonde, dressed out of all proportion to the place with a silver brocade dress and silver mules, sat next to Valcanas and kept blowing a contrary lock of silvery-white hair away from her right eye. Valcanas's bandage over his eye had been reduced to a wide Band-Aid.

"Mind if I sit down, Mo?" Balzic said.

"If you're dumb enough to want the company of a wide-awake drunk, who am I to deny you the pleasure?" Valcanas said. "Excuse me. Almost forgot my manners. Mario Balzic, this is, uh, what's your name again, dear?"

"Cindy," the blonde said, huffing again at the lock of hair.

"That's it. Cindy. All you have to think of is cinders."

"Hi," Cindy said. "Can I have another drink?"

"Cinders, *may* you have another drink," Valcanas said.

"May I—can I—I'd like another drink, okay?"

"Charming girl," Valcanas said to Balzic. "Illiterate, but charming."

"So who gets a charge out of reading books? I hated school."

"There, Mario, is a jump in logic not even Freud would have tried to explain. Louis, my good man, bring my charming friend here two of whatever she's drinking," Valcanas called out in the general direction of the bar. "And now, Mario, what can I do for you that you think I ought to, but which we both know I would be infinitely better off not doing?"

"It's, uh, Tina Samarra. You remember. The butcher's sister."

"You're not going to get me another client for crissake. I've got seven right now I don't want."

"Six, dearie," Cindy said. "I can take a hint."

"Sit down and drink your drinks. It's a sin to waste good booze. Besides, you didn't have anything to do with hiring me. Your boy friend did. And he's the only one who can fire me. So just be a good girl and shut up. You know—close your mouth and let your natural charm reveal itself."

"This one needs a lawyer, Mo," Balzic said.

"They all need lawyers. What am I? The only lawyer left?"

"Well, you know about the case."

"You mean that one about the butcher who got himself butchered?"

"I wish to hell you'd put it a little different, but, yes, that's the one."

"You mean she did it?"

Balzic nodded.

"And you want *me* to defend *her?* A female hacks a guy in little pieces and you want me to defend her. Mario, where the hell's your sense of proportion? I should be on the other side."

"That's not all she did," Balzic said. After thinking a long moment, he added, "I figure this guy rated it."

"Listen, Cinders," Valcanas said, "take a walk for five minutes. I want to talk to this man privately. And I said walk. That means you stay upright and keep going places. That doesn't mean you keep moving with your feet on the floor."

"Boy, are you ever funny. Where'd Anthony ever find you?" Cindy picked up both her drinks and sauntered off toward the bar.

"She kills me," Valcanas said. "She keeps calling Digs DiLisi Anthony. She thinks he's going to send her to New York. To appear on Broadway, no less. She'll make a hell of a lot of appearances, all right, but there won't be any stage."

"So what's she up for? Rehearsing on her own time?"

"Something like that," Valcanas said, grinning. "Let's get back to this other female—what's her name again?"

"Tina Samarra."

"That's it. Now you said you figured the guy rated it. Did you say that, or am I just getting that impression from the righteousness on your face? Mario, no shit, you have to do something about that. It's boring as hell to have to look at the countenance of a moral defender all the time."

"Yeah, sure. In the first place, I did say it. The guy did rate it as far as I'm concerned. He gave her the best reason any woman could have." Balzic went on to explain, bringing Valcanas up to date in every detail. "So what do you think?" he said finally. "Is it worth your time?"

"That depends how much I get paid—if I get paid."

"Oh, her brother'll pay you. Don't sweat that. But what do you think? I mean, what'll she get?"

"Well, we plead her guilty. I call three witnesses, her and those two her boy friend went fishing with—among other things—and the only tricky part will be making sure those two don't know she burned all the movies. Otherwise, from what you say, they'd have everything to gain by shutting up."

"Both of us together can take care of that," Balzic said. "I just keep them locked up until you talk to somebody in the DA's office to tell somebody else to set their bond so high nobody'll take a chance on getting walked on it. So then, if you ask all the questions as though the movies are still around, what's the problem?"

"None. There won't be any."

"So what do you think she'll get?"

"That depends on the judge. I'll get it set up in front of Koerner. He's a good, proper Lutheran. He'll be duly horrified. I'd say she'll get eleven to twenty-three months. Good behavior, hell, she'll be out in a year."

Balzic frowned.

"What the hell do you want for crissake? I mean, what the hell, Mario, she's got to do a little time. You know, she's got to reflect upon the error of her ways. The least she can do is spend a year thinking about who she shacks up with from now on."

"I don't know," Balzic said, "seems almost a shame she has to do any time at all."

"Mario, what you need is a drink," Valcanas said. "Louis, a drink for my friend here. The world is too much with him, late and soon."

"What did you say? The world is too much what?"

"The world is too much with you, late and soon," Valcanas said. "That's Wordsworth. You know, poetry. Christ, why am I surrounded by illiterates? I have to start loafing in better saloons."

"If you don't mind, Mo, just save the poetry," Balzic said. "I'll take the drink."

And he did. Many of them.